Just About Forever

By Leanne Gelish

Dedicated to my husband- in every love story, I fall in love with you.

Copyright Disclaimer

Chapter One

It's a grey, gloomy day on Long Island—the kind where the air feels thick with nostalgia and the streets glisten with the aftermath of last night's rain. I'm tucked away in the corner of a cozy bookstore café, my laptop open, fingers drumming absentmindedly against the keys. A year ago, I never would've pictured myself here— settled, engaged, living in Huntington, of all places. But here I am. And against all odds, I'm happy.

Moving back felt like a gamble. I'd spent years dodging the suburban pull, convinced that if I stayed in the city long enough, I'd stumble into some grand, cinematic version of my life. But I've realized something lately—maybe happiness isn't about grandness. Maybe it's about the quiet, everyday moments: the way the barista at my usual café knows my order, the way the salty air from the harbor smells in the morning, the way Brian pulls me closer in his sleep.

I take a sip of my coffee—strong and slightly bitter—and glance around. This bookstore café is new to me, but it already feels like the kind of place I could waste hours in: writing, people-watching, and eavesdropping on the occasional conversation. It's the kind of place that makes you want to romanticize your own life. So, naturally, I've decided it's a sign. Serendipity at its finest.

Tonight, I have an open mic, and instead of preparing, I'm procrastinating. At twenty-six, I've dabbled in more career paths than I can count. I've resisted the *"traditional path"* like it's the plague—chasing passions, avoiding the corporate grind. It hasn't been easy, but honestly? I love it. Stand-up comedy feels like the perfect blend of everything I am: the writer, the performer, the observer. It's my way of making sense of the world—of turning all the awkward, uncomfortable moments into something funny. Sure, most of my gigs are unpaid, and I'm still waitressing to cover rent, but even on the worst days, I wouldn't trade it for anything.

I tap at the keyboard, smiling as my latest joke comes to life:

My mom found my rabbit the other day. And no, I'm not talking about a fluffy pet—this one's battery-operated.
She looked at me like I'd brought home a felony.
It's funny, because if I were a guy and she found a sock under my bed, it'd be "boys will be boys."
But a woman with a vibrator? Suddenly it's "we need to talk."
Look, I'm not here to stand on a feminist soapbox, but I will say this: WO-MEN MAS-TER-BATE.
And here's the kicker, folks—we actually know where it is.

I chuckle, satisfied. It's bold—but that's the point. If comedy has taught me anything, it's that discomfort is where the best laughs come from.

Before I can bask in my comedic genius too long, my phone buzzes.

Brian.

The sight of his name makes me smile.

"Hey, baby," I answer, leaning back in my chair. "How's your day?"

"It's good. Just wanted to check if you're coming to the dinner tonight."

My stomach drops. "Oh, crap. I forgot! I have an open mic, but—"

"Char, I know you love comedy, but this dinner is important." His voice is gentle, but I know what he's really saying.

"And so is this. Look, I'll figure it out. What time is the dinner?"

"It's at six, in Melville."

"Perfect. The open mic doesn't start till nine. See? Both our worlds can live in harmony."

He laughs. "Only you, Char."

"Exactly. Have a good rest of your day. I love you."

"Love you, too."

Three months from now, we'll be married. That still feels surreal to say. I glance down at my engagement ring—a two-carat princess cut that sparkles even in the dim café light. It still feels new, like something I'm playing dress-up with. But it's real. We're real.

Brian and I grew up on Long Island. He went to Chaminade, I went to Mercy—your quintessential Catholic school pairing. We reconnected nine months ago in the most fate-like way possible: me, mid-stand-up set at a Manhattan bar, locking eyes with him and blurting out, "Hey, I know you! You're the guy I gave a handy to at the ninth-grade Chaminade dance."
His face had turned bright red, but it was the best icebreaker of my life. And now—here we are. Engaged.

I sigh contentedly, stretch, and scroll through my phone. A quick Facebook check turns into a full-blown scroll spiral through the lives of people I barely talk to anymore. I'm about to close the app when a message notification pops up.

Hey bird, how are you?

I freeze.

There's only one person who ever called me *bird*. And I haven't heard from him in seven years.

Hunter Maisley.

First love. First heartbreak. First person who ever really got me—or at least, that's how it felt. Even now, I can't untangle what we were. I just know it took me a long time to stop looking for him in crowded rooms. Before I can talk myself out of it, I type a response.

Charlotte: Um, hi?

The typing bubble appears immediately. My stomach flips.

Hunter: I know, it's been a minute. I saw a video of you on YouTube and was so pumped you're doing comedy. You're a natural. Figured I'd reach out before you're too famous to remember us little people.

I reread it twice, unsure if I want to laugh or scream. That's the thing about Hunter—he always knew how to make me feel both at once.

Charlotte: A minute? More like 3,679,200 minutes! Lol. I can't believe you saw one of my videos 😬 I've been at it for about a year, and I'm obsessed. Just finished my set for tonight when I got your message.

The typing bubbles pop up again, but this time, I don't feel anxious.

Hunter: You really need to stop watching *Rent* on repeat... Did you seriously sing "525,600 minutes" until you calculated seven years?
But seriously, the video was hilarious. The bit about your dad's Facebook rants had me in tears.

I laugh out loud. "Don't knock *Rent*, Maisley—it's a classic. That video's a hit with everyone but my parents, lol. What have you been up to?"

Hunter: Bird, you definitely didn't exaggerate your mom's accent. Do you remember when she used to visit us in college?

I grin. A real, genuine, feel-it-in-your-stomach kind of grin.

"I do. And I remember you making fun of it the whole time."

The clock on my laptop reads 4:45. I sigh.

Charlotte: I hate to cut this short, but I have to walk Franny before dinner and my gig. Well, "gig" —it's a free open mic, but let's call it a gig. Text me? My number's 516-543-2112.

A few seconds later, my phone buzzes.

Hunter: I never deleted your number. I'd love to keep talking, too.

And just like that, Hunter Maisley is back in my life.

Chapter Two

A few weeks into the suburban life, and the shiny-new-car feeling is already wearing off.

Adjusting to a new life hasn't been as easy as I thought. I've always been the kind of person who looks for the silver lining, the brighter side of things. I pride myself on it, actually. When I moved to Huntington, I told myself it was a new adventure—a new house, a new town, a chance to build something real with Brian. And for a while, I believed it.

I marveled at the charm of our neighborhood, at the way the hydrangeas bloomed wildly in front yards, how the smell of the bay drifted inland when the wind shifted. I loved how Franny had a sprawling backyard to explore, how she raced in happy circles every morning.

I told myself I was lucky. Not many people get handed a house—a beautiful, classic colonial with white shutters and a wraparound porch—just waiting to be filled with memories. Directly across the street from one of the largest parks in the area. It's a beautiful gift.

And I am lucky. But lately, something feels... off. Like I've slipped into someone else's life, playing a role I don't remember auditioning for.

I go through the motions: walk Franny in the mornings, grab coffee at the same café where the barista now knows my order, try to busy myself with wedding planning and writing. But there's this underlying sense of detachment, like I'm watching my own life play out from the outside— pressing my hands against the glass but never quite breaking through.

It's the same conversation on repeat.
What shade of ivory do you want for the linens?
Did you confirm the band?
Have you sent out the RSVP reminders?

Brian's mother calls every other day with updates on the wedding, each one feeling less like mine. And Brian—he's been so caught up in work, in the grind of becoming a CPA, that when we do see each other, we talk logistics. Budgets. Guest lists.

Plans for a life that feels increasingly like it was mapped out *for* me instead of *by* me.

I should feel more excited. I should feel something other than this floating, simulation-like existence, where everything is perfect in theory but slightly wrong in practice—like a dream where the setting is familiar but the details don't quite make sense.

The only time I feel real lately is when I'm talking to Hunter.

I never expected us to fall back into such an easy rhythm. But somehow, we have. Our conversations are sharp and fun and effortless—the kind that shake me awake from this haze of Stepford Wives. Okay, maybe that's a little dramatic... but sometimes, my life feels so... created for me.

Talking to Hunter is a tether to something I can't quite name, but it reminds me of myself—of who I was before all of this. Before wedding dresses and dinner parties and long, lonely nights in a house that still doesn't feel like mine.

Four months ago, I never would've imagined this.

We were still in our cramped Queens apartment when Brian came home with an envelope in his hand. I was working on a new set, trying to decide if my depression jokes would make an audience uncomfortable, when he leaned down and kissed my forehead.

"Babe, we need to talk," he said.

My stomach clenched. I set my laptop aside, bracing for the worst.

Instead, he handed me the envelope. "My parents sent this. I opened it at the office. You need to see what's inside." I tipped the envelope, and a key slid into my hand. Its tag read: *35 Primrose Street, Huntington NY. Welcome Home.*

Brian grinned like a kid on Christmas morning. "My parents bought us a house," he said, practically bouncing. "It's right across from the park, Char. Sure, the commute will be longer for me, but—we have a house!"

He kissed me again, but I couldn't move.

Long Island?

I'd just signed up for UCB comedy classes. My entire life was in the city. I wanted to tell him how I felt, but the look on his face—the pure, unfiltered excitement—made me swallow my doubts.

How could I be so selfish when the entire point of getting married is to build something *together*? We'd end up in the suburbs anyway, right? Why not now?

"Franny," I whispered, scratching behind her ear, "looks like you're getting that backyard you've always wanted."

Within a week, I'd gotten my money back from UCB—thanks to a little white lie about a death in the family—and we were packed up and moving in. We took hundreds of pictures that day. All three of us wedged into the front seat of the moving van. I even set the camera up for a self-timer shot at the front door, which turned out even better when Franny leapt into our arms at the last second.

It was idyllic. It was beautiful.

It still is, I guess. The house is beautiful, but it doesn't feel like mine. Brian is thriving—working long hours, making plans for our future. Meanwhile, I'm floating. Trying to find my place in a town that feels like an elaborate movie set where I'm playing the role of *future wife* but keep forgetting my lines.

I don't tell Brian how lonely I've been. How, despite my best efforts, I feel more like a guest in my own life. How the weight of other people's expectations is starting to suffocate me.

I don't tell him that the only relief I've found has been in my conversations with Hunter.

Hunter, who always knew how to ground me— even when I didn't realize I was drifting. Hunter, who has his own complicated life: his long-term relationship with Kelly, who, from my online stalking, looks like she has it all figured out. He told me things with her aren't perfect. That she wants to get married and he doesn't. That she gave up a lot to be with him, and he's not sure he'll ever be able to give her what she wants.

I don't know what it's like to have someone give up everything for me. But I do know what it's like to weigh my own dreams against someone else's.

This morning, while walking Franny through the park, my phone buzzes.

Hunter: Would it be crazy to meet up before your wedding?

I stop mid-step, Franny tugging on her leash as she sniffs a patch of wildflowers. My heart skips a beat. Would it be crazy? Probably. Before I can overthink it, another message comes in.

Hunter: I'm going to be in Albany next weekend. My sister just had a baby, so I'm heading up to visit my parents.

I stare at the screen, blinking.

Charlotte: No way. I'm going to be in Albany next weekend too. There's a gig I've been trying to get mic time at—a tiny hole-in-the-wall theater hosting a comedy showcase.

Hunter: Kismet. Or fate. Or just dumb luck. Either way—should we get coffee?

The thing about Hunter—about our past—is that it's unsettled. I've buried that feeling deep down, in a part of my heart with a locked door. To be fair, I'm not even sure what Hunter and I ever were... or what we are now. There's always been a comfort in our conversations—there *always* was. From the first time we met in college, it just felt easy. And that kind of thing doesn't always happen.

But he destroyed that. And now I've let him back into my life. I try not to think too hard about it. Sure, we've found a comfortable rhythm again, but it's dancing on the surface of something deeper. Something unfinished. For seven years, I've wanted closure. To know why we ended the way we did. To understand if it ever meant as much to him as it did to me. And now, the idea of seeing him again—of facing whatever it is that still lingers between us—sets my nerves on fire.

No. That what-if belongs in another life. Another version of me. This is just two old friends catching up. That's all. I sit down on a park bench, watching the geese glide across the pond as I rub Franny's belly. My fingers hover over the screen, hesitating for just a second before I type:

Charlotte: Irongate? 9:30?

I hit send, exhale sharply, and watch the three dots of anxiety appear on my screen.

I should feel nervous. I should feel guilty. I should be considering that I'm self sabotaging.

But all I feel is awake.

Chapter Three

The coffee shop is warm, cozy, and entirely too small for the weight sitting on my chest. I arrived fifteen minutes early, even though I told myself I wouldn't. I picked a table by the window, thinking it would make me feel less trapped. Now, I regret it. Sitting here in plain view, I feel like a character in someone else's story—one where everyone passing by can see straight through me. Like they know I'm waiting for a man who doesn't belong in my present.

My hands curl around my cup. It's too hot, but I don't let go. The heat anchors me, grounding me in something tangible. I focus on the weight of the ceramic, on the slow swirl of steam curling into the air—anything to keep me from looking at the door.

I shouldn't be this nervous. But I am. Because this is Hunter Maisley.

The last time I saw him, I was nineteen. I was walking away from the boy who shattered me, trying to convince myself I'd be okay. And yet here I am—waiting for him like no time has passed at all.

I glance at my phone, rereading our texts like I need proof this is really happening. Like I need to remind myself that this is just two old friends catching up. That's all. But my body doesn't feel like it believes me. Because some people never really leave you, not all the way.

The bell over the door chimes, and I forget how to breathe. Hunter walks in like he owns the place—like he isn't seven years late. His eyes scan the café, searching. Then he finds me.

Our eyes lock. And he smiles.

Like nothing ever happened. Like we're still eighteen and there hasn't been a whole life—a whole heartbreak—between us. My heart sinks to my butthole. Graphic, maybe. But you know the feeling.

He moves toward me, casual, effortless. I hate that I remember exactly how he walks. The slight swing in his step, the way his shoulders relax like the world has always bent a little in his favor. I hate that I still notice the way his jaw tenses before he smiles—just a half-second pause, like he's waiting to see how I'll react.

The air between us tightens. I grip my cup a little harder as he reaches my table.

"Hey, bird."

His voice is deeper now, rougher, but the way he says it—like it's still an inside joke, like we're still teasing each other in the dorm common room—stirs something in my chest. He smells the same, and I hate that too. Something clean and familiar. The kind of scent that sneaks up on you and pulls memories from places you thought you'd buried.

I swallow hard. "How do you remember that nickname?"

His mouth lifts at the corner. "I still remember a lot of things."

I don't ask what things. I don't want to know. Not right now.

Instead, I nod toward the seat across from me. "Sit."

He does. And for a moment, neither of us says anything. Seven years of silence. And yet, it's not awkward. It's just... there. This weight. This thing between us that never really left.

I clear my throat. "So... YouTube, huh?"

His grin returns. "Yeah. You did a whole bit about your mom finding your vibrator. I almost choked on my drink."

A laugh escapes before I can stop it. "Oh God. *That* one?"

"Oh yeah. The way you compared it to a guy's sock? Perfect."

I shake my head, both amused and slightly mortified. "That was one of the first jokes I wrote that really landed. I knew it was risky, but I figured if people laughed at *that*, I was onto something."

"You were. Stand-up suits you." His voice is softer now.

I shrug, shifting under his gaze. "I like it. It's honest. I don't have to be anyone but myself up there."

Something flickers in his expression, but it's gone before I can name it.

"And Brian?" he asks, casually, like it's just another part of catching up. "You're getting married in a few weeks?"

I should've expected it. But hearing Brian's name from Hunter's mouth—it doesn't sound right. Like it doesn't belong in the same room with us.

I nod, forcing a small smile. "Yeah. In four weeks."

Hunter watches me for a moment, gaze steady. "You happy?"

It's such a simple question. Too simple. And yet my answer takes a beat too long to come.

"Of course."

It's not a lie. But it's not the whole truth either. Because happiness isn't something I've thought about lately—not in a big, *Hunter-Maisley-is-sitting-across-from-me-and-making-me-question*-everything kind of way.

His eyes linger on mine like he can tell. Like he knows. And I hate that he still knows me this well.

I shift, trying to shake the tension. "I *am* happy, don't get me wrong. But the pressure of the wedding, the expectations from our parents, from him—while also trying to carve out my own path—it's a lot. It's like... will I have to lose myself to fit into the mold? I'm sure it's just pre-wedding jitters or whatever, but sometimes it all feels a little unreal. Like a simulation."

Hunter tilts his head, considering. "I don't know you in this phase of life. But the Charlotte I remember? She always beat to her own drum.

Maybe it's not unhappiness you're feeling. Maybe it's just the challenge of learning how to beat along with someone else."

I sip my coffee, taking in his words. He's always had this way of offering the exact insight I don't want to hear—but somehow need. And he never says it with judgment. Just... knowing.

"For what it's worth," he adds, "it sounds like Brian appreciates you for who you are. That's the most important thing in any relationship."

I nod, but his words settle heavily in my chest. Because Brian *does* appreciate me. He's never tried to change me.

The problem is, I'm not sure I know who I am anymore.

We talk for the next hour. Not about what happened. Not about Fiona. Not about why we haven't spoken in seven years. We talk about his job, my stand-up, small things that circle the bigger thing we don't dare say out loud. And maybe that's the most telling part of all.

Because I should want to ask him. I should want to say: *Why did you keep me a secret? Why did I have to find out about her that way? Why didn't you fight for me?*

But I don't.

Because I don't want the answers.And I don't want to ruin whatever *this* is—this small, suspended moment where we exist in the same space again. It feels good. Maybe too good.

The coffee shop starts to empty. The late afternoon quiet settles in.

Hunter watches me, then says, "Walk with me?"

I glance at my phone. Brian's name lights up the screen. A reminder. A boundary. A promise.

And yet, when I look up, Hunter is watching me like he already knows the answer.

I exhale slowly, pushing away the part of me that knows better.

But instead—

I nod.

And just like that, I step further into the fire.

Chapter Four

Outside, the air is crisp, sharp in a way that makes me feel alive.

Albany in the fall has always felt like a secret—a city caught between worlds. The old stone buildings press against the sky, their windows glowing with the warmth of coffee shops and bookstores. Leaves scatter in the streets, spinning in little whirlwinds before settling in uneven piles along the sidewalks.

Hunter and I walk in step, our breath visible in the cold air. Neither of us speaks right away, but it doesn't feel awkward. Just... expectant.

I wrap my arms around myself, inhaling the scent of damp pavement and distant bonfires. I shouldn't be here.

But I am.

Hunter has his hands tucked into the pockets of his coat, his gaze flicking around like he's remembering things too. Like this place belongs to both of us.

And maybe it does.

We pass the Empire State Plaza, where the reflection of the city stretches across the still water of the pools. The Capitol looms ahead, its stone steps grand, the kind of place that makes you feel small.

I slow near the statue of the suffragettes—three women cast in bronze, their faces set in defiant determination.

"I used to sit here after class sometimes," I say, surprising myself. "Just thinking. Or pretending to study."

Hunter smirks. "Or avoiding people?"

I exhale a laugh. "You know me too well."

A gust of wind pushes past us, lifting strands of my hair across my face. I tuck them behind my ear, catching the way his gaze lingers.

Like he's seeing something he wasn't ready for.

Like this is hurting him, too.

We keep walking, turning down a side street lined with brownstones and memories I haven't let myself think about in years.

"I missed this," Hunter says quietly.

I glance at him. "Albany?"

He shakes his head. "You."

I feel that in my bones.

But I don't respond. Because I don't know how.

Instead, I find myself thinking back to when this all was the most important thing in the world.

Seven Years Ago

At Smith College, I was always running from something.

Freshman year, it was my family, my hometown, the expectations that felt too suffocating. I fell into a new life quickly. My roommate, Effie Richards, was a breath of fresh air. We clicked instantly, and within 48 hours, we were inseparable—something that has continued to this day.

Effie had this ability to make quick friends, and in college, she did this with the boys on the bottom floor—the same floor Hunter lived on and supervised.

Hunter was the junior Resident Assistant for the freshmen. Technically, he was off-limits to all of us, and in the beginning, we didn't pay him much mind. Our group of friends—Sean, Austen, and Josh—was always together. We pushed curfew often, sneaking into bars with fake IDs, ending the nights in dorm common rooms with cheap beer and oversharing.

At some point, Hunter started joining us. He used the excuse that he was trying to keep us out of trouble, but Effie always suspected it was because he had a crush on me.

One night, while studying in the library alone, I received a text from a 585 number.

Hey, it's Hunter. I hope you don't mind—I got your number from Sean.

My heart skipped two beats.

Effie might have clocked his crush on me, but what she didn't know was that the feeling was mutual. From the second I saw him on check-in day, I was drawn to him. It only got stronger the more I got to know him.

I texted back almost too quickly.

Hey, I don't mind at all.

Cool. Where are you? The gang is ordering Domino's, and it's not the same without you.

My heart panged. I wanted to be with them, but I was also supposed to be studying. Except—I wasn't studying at all. I was writing a skit for an open mic night off campus. My parents insisted I get a degree, and I was, but that didn't mean I couldn't chase comedy too.

Oh dang, I'm in the library.

Silence. An hour passed. I kept checking my phone, waiting for a reply that never came.

And then—I felt him.

I glanced up, and there he was.

"Since you couldn't join us, I thought I'd join you."

He set a box of cheesy bread on the table.

And that was it.

In the beginning, we were just friends. Late-night studying in the library, sneaking off to empty classrooms to talk about everything and nothing, lingering too long in the back seats of cars after group outings. It was unspoken, but it was there—the pull, the gravity, the inevitability of it all.

Effie assumed something was going on pretty early. She was witchy that way. I never even had to tell her.

"You and Hunter are a thing, huh?" she had asked one night, twirling a piece of gum between her fingers.

"We're not a thing," I had said, too quickly.

She had just smirked. "Not yet."

Things shifted between Hunter and me during Effie's birthday trip to Lake George right before finals. Effie thought she was being clever when she put Hunter and me in the Romeo and Juliet room.

The house was ridiculous—massive, sprawling, the kind of place no group of college kids should have had access to. Indoor pool, hot tub, a fully stocked kitchen. Effie's parents had spared no expense for her birthday weekend.

The night had been a blur of too many tacos, too many margaritas, and tequila shots we definitely didn't need. By the time I crawled into bed, the world had stopped spinning, but there was a warmth in my body, a looseness.

And then—the knock.

Three soft taps against the wooden door.

I blinked, sleep fogging my brain as I sat up, pushing my hair from my face.

Another knock.

I swung my legs over the side of the bed, my feet hitting the cold hardwood floor as I padded to the door. I barely hesitated before cracking it open, and there he was.

Hunter.

Not drunk. Not wobbly or flushed like he had been earlier. Just him. Awake. Sober. Standing in the dim glow of the hallway, one hand pressed against the doorframe.

"Want to watch a movie?" he asked, voice low.

I should've said no. I should've laughed, rolled my eyes, told him to go to bed. But I didn't.Because the truth was, I wasn't drunk anymore either, and it was nice to have some company.

I stepped aside without a word.

He climbed onto the bed beside me, close enough that I could feel the heat of him, even though we weren't touching.

"Mrs. Doubtfire?" I asked, scrolling through Netflix.

A slow grin spread across his face. "Classic."

The movie started, and it felt awkward at first. I was nervous, maybe he was too. I felt like I was holding my breath. At some point, his leg pressed against mine. I inched closer, even being brave enough to rest my head on his shoulder.

At the scene where Robin Williams becomes a woman, I leap to my feet and belt "Don't Rain on My Parade" with the TV, full Streisand arms and all. Hunter is half-laughing, half-groaning, muttering something about regretting every life choice that brought him here. I collapse back onto the bed, breathless and grinning, turning toward him to make a joke—

And then his mouth is on mine.

There's nothing tentative about it. No fumbling, no hesitation. Just heat. His hands grip my waist like he's starved for this—for me—pulling me flush against him, and I can feel it. Him. Hard and heavy against my thigh, the thick press of his cock through his jeans making my entire body thrum.

The taste of tequila and nerves and three months of unspoken tension explodes between us. My fingers fist in his shirt, tugging, needing, gasping as his tongue parts my lips and deepens the kiss. One hand slides beneath my sweater, palm hot and deliberate against my stomach, dragging upward until his thumb brushes under the swell of my breast.

"Fuck," he breathes, low and wrecked, "you're so goddamn soft."

I'm already wet. Throbbing. Aching with every second he doesn't touch me where I need it most. When he shifts, I feel the thick line of his cock rub against me, and I moan into his mouth like it's instinct.

"Are you sure?" he asks, voice tight, forehead pressed against mine.

I nod, my hands already yanking at the hem of his shirt. "Yes. Please."

He doesn't make me ask twice. My sweater is gone in seconds, his mouth trailing heat down my neck, over my collarbone, between my breasts. I claw at his belt, desperate now, and when he finally pushes my leggings down and touches me—really touches me—I cry out.

"God, you're soaked," he groans, two fingers sliding between my folds. "You've been like this for me all night, haven't you?"

I can't speak. I can only nod, hips rocking toward his hand, chasing the friction like I'll die without it. He presses a finger inside me, then another, curling just right, watching my face like he's memorizing every reaction.

And then—he replaces them with the thick, hot length of him. He pushes in slow, inch by torturous inch, his cock stretching me, filling me in a way that has my mouth dropping open in a silent gasp.

"Jesus Christ," he grits out, burying his face in my neck as he bottoms out. "You feel like fucking heaven."

I wrap my legs around him, nails digging into his back, completely lost to the rhythm of his hips, the sound of skin on skin, the heat and the sweat and the way we fall apart—together. The movie keeps playing, casting flickering shadows against the walls, but it doesn't matter.

The only thing I know is this: his body, my body, the way he moves inside me like we've done this a thousand times. Like he's always known how to make me come undone.

And when I do—when it crashes over me like fire —I scream his name.

After that weekend, we were addicted.

The secret had always been fun—sneaking glances across rooms, brushing fingers in passing, pretending not to feel the magnetic pull between us. But after that night, there was no pretending. No going back.

We were insatiable.

If we were alone, we touched. If we had five minutes, we used them. 3 a.m. in empty common rooms. Pressed against dorm walls, my back scraping brick, his hand up my skirt. In his car, fogging up windows while I rode him, muffling moans against his neck. Library study rooms with locked doors and quiet gasps. His bed. Mine. Desks, couches, doorways.

Anywhere we could get lost in each other, we did.

Hunter was a drug I couldn't quit—and I didn't want to. He made me reckless. He made me bold. With him, all my cynicism about love, about men, about forever—it disappeared. Not because I believed in fairy tales, but because I believed in him.

He saw me. Understood me before I spoke. Showed up to my off-campus comedy sets like I was already famous. Pulled me out of panic spirals with a single look. Listened. Really listened.

And when he touched me, it wasn't just sex. It was claiming. Worship. Need. Every time he slid inside me, it felt like something holy. Like I was made for him. Like he was made for me.

But we kept it quiet. Always quiet.

Because of Sean. Because Hunter said it was easier that way. Sean had asked me out earlier in the semester, and he was Hunter's roommate, so... it was messy. Or, that's what I told myself every time I wanted to post a picture on MySpace. Every time I wanted to tell Effie everything.

So we stayed silent.

In front of our friends, we razzed each other like enemies. Sat on opposite sides of rooms. Flirted with other people so no one would suspect how obsessed we were behind closed doors.

But when the doors shut—when it was just us— we were feral. Clothes hit the floor. Mouths collided. Our bodies tangled until we forgot our own names. I memorized the sounds he made. He memorized the way I came.

On the weekends, when Sean stayed at his childhood home a few blocks from campus, we snuck into his empty room and acted like we lived there. Pretending it was ours. Pretending we could keep doing this forever.

It was everything.

We even made plans for summer—me visiting him in Rochester, him coming down to Long Island to see the ocean for the first time. He wanted to swim with me under the stars. He told me he loved the idea of water that went on forever.

But forever never came.

Because one day, everything changed.

I was on my way to class, taking the same back stairwell I always used. I planned to meet Sean downstairs. I pushed the door open, already texting—

And froze.

There he was.

Hunter. With a girl.

Her name was Fiona. A junior. I recognized her from the dorm mixers. She was pretty in the way that looked curated—like someone who never got messy, never got real.

They were kissing.

I didn't move. My brain couldn't catch up. Maybe I misread it. Maybe it was one of his cover-up moves, trying to steer attention away from us. Maybe it was nothing. We'd flirted a little too hard the night before. Maybe he was overcorrecting.

But then—

Her arms wrapped tighter around his neck. His hand dropped to her back. Not fumbling. Not uncertain. Just... familiar.

Like he'd done it a hundred times before. Like it had always been her.

I stood there, frozen, my heart pounding in my throat, waiting for him to look up. Waiting for him to see me. To flinch. To pull away. To do something—anything—to show I wasn't a secret. That I mattered. That we mattered.

But he didn't.

He leaned in— And kissed her again.

Now

The street narrows, the city quieter here. The hum of cars and distant conversations fades, like another life. Hunter breaks the silence.

"I was an idiot back then," he says.

I stop walking.

He turns to face me, expression unreadable. "I should've told you about Fiona. I should've told you everything."

"Yeah," I manage, swallowing hard. "You should have."

He exhales, rubs a hand over his jaw. "We were hiding us, and I got tired of it. Dating her was supposed to be easy. It wasn't. It was the worst decision of my life."

Tears well. "You dating her was the worst experience of mine, too."

"I loved you, Charlotte."

The words punch through me.

I almost laugh—anything to keep from sobbing. "No, you didn't."

His jaw flexes. "I did." He steps closer, testing an invisible boundary. When I don't move, he moves again. His breath slides over my cheek, and every system in my body spikes.

His hands lift, thumbs brushing fresh tears from my skin. I should pull away. I don't. Heat coils low in my belly as his fingers trace my jaw, tilting my chin.

He kisses me.

Soft, searching—then greedy. His palms lock on my hips and tug me flush, hard length unmistakable against me. I fist his shirt, holding on while the world blurs. His mouth—warm, familiar, addictive—consumes me until a slow burn becomes an inferno.

I sigh into him; he swallows the sound like it's his right. Woodsy, clean Hunter wraps around me, drowning everything but this.

Time doesn't exist—only the press of lips, the slick heat of tongues, the way my body molds to his like it's the most natural thing on earth.

When we finally break apart, foreheads touching, our breaths tangle. Hearts pound in sync, confessing truths we still can't say.

My phone buzzes.

I freeze. Hunter stays close while I fumble it out.

Brian: *Are you coming home soon? Dinner's at eight. It's important I show I'm a family man, Char. This determines our future.*

Reality slams into me. Brian—my fiancé. Four weeks from now, I'm supposed to marry him.

I step back. Hunter's hands fall, but his eyes don't.

"I—I have to go." I dig for my keys, brain scrambling. It's only three; I can make it home, pretend this never—

"Don't marry him, Char," he says, voice low but solid.

The words strike like a match. I grip my keys, throat thick. "I don't know if I can."
I'm not sure if I mean walking away from Brian— or walking away from Hunter.

This is a mistake. I know it even as I let it happen. I turn, forcing my feet toward the life I promised to build. The rest—I'll figure out later.

Chapter Five

The dinner is elegant. White tablecloths, dim lighting, the scent of expensive wine lingering in the air. It's the kind of place where people talk in hushed, measured tones, where laughter is never too loud, where everything is curated to make you feel important.

Brian is in his element.

I am not.

I lift my wine glass to my lips, smiling at the appropriate times, nodding in all the right places. I play my role effortlessly—the perfect wife-to-be, the woman who fits seamlessly into his world.

But inside, I feel like I'm drifting. Like I'm watching myself from above, some version of me who knows exactly how to behave, exactly what to say, exactly when to laugh.

I tell myself this is the life I signed up for. This is what it meant when I happily exclaimed yes to Brian's proposal. His life will always be dinners and impressions. My role will always be the supportive wife at his side. His anchor, as he so often calls me.

This dinner is just another scene in the life I agreed to.

And yet—I barely taste the wine. I barely hear Brian's voice as he leans in, murmuring something about making a good impression.

I nod, because I'm supposed to nod. I smile, because I'm supposed to smile. But in my mind, I'm somewhere else. Not here. Not at this table, surrounded by talk of hedge funds and market trends. Not in this restaurant, where every moment feels rehearsed.

I am mentally in a time loop, reliving the past four hours.

Hunter's lips. Hunter's hands. Hunter's voice, steady and certain. "Don't marry him, Char."

I lift my glass, my fingers tightening around the stem, and take a sip of wine I can't taste. And for the first time, I wonder if I'm already too far gone to turn back.

Four hours ago, I wasn't in a simulation mimicked after Stepford Wives.

Four hours ago, I was standing in the middle of an Albany street, the cold air biting at my cheeks, the city buzzing faintly in the background. I was wrapped in the smell of damp pavement and firewood, the weight of Hunter's hands still on my face, the ghost of his mouth still lingering on mine.

I was alive.

I wasn't smiling because I was supposed to.

I wasn't nodding because it was expected.

I was just there. Fully in the moment. Fully in myself.

And it wasn't just about Hunter—I know that. It wasn't just about the way his lips felt on mine, or the way my body instinctively folded into his like it had been waiting for that moment for years.

It was about something deeper. Something I haven't let myself feel in a long time.

It was freedom.

For the first time in years, I wasn't thinking about what came next. I wasn't performing. I wasn't playing the role of someone's future wife or the responsible woman who had her life figured out.

I was just Charlotte.

And now, here I am, sitting in a high-end restaurant, back in the life I've spent years carefully curating—the one that's supposed to be the dream.

Then why does it feel so hollow?

"Charlotte?"

Brian's voice pulls me back. I blink, realizing his boss is looking at me expectantly, waiting for an answer to a question I didn't hear.

"Sorry," I say quickly, pasting on an apologetic smile. "What was that?"

Brian shifts beside me, a flicker of tension in his jaw.

His boss chuckles, indulgent. "I was just asking how wedding planning is going. Brian tells us you've been balancing a lot lately."

"Ah." I clear my throat, smoothing my napkin over my lap. "Yes, it's been... a process. But it's coming together."

A lie.

I haven't looked at a seating chart or a catering list in weeks—Brian's mom calls, says something, and I agree. Because, does it really matter where Aunt Shelley sits? Do I really care if the chicken has asparagus or mashed potatoes? I should be poring over floral arrangements, obsessing over linen swatches, picking the perfect entrée for the reception. That's what brides do.

Instead, I've been writing. Filming. Applying to roles, chasing stand-up gigs, doing anything and everything to hold onto the pieces of myself that still feel real. The truth is, I don't care about the wedding as much as I should.

I should be excited. I should be glowing, gushing about the dress, the flowers, the honeymoon.

Instead, I just nod, forcing another smile. Brian's hand finds my knee under the table. A silent warning. Stay present.

I swallow the lump in my throat and take another sip of wine. I get through the rest of the dinner with polite nods, a few quick jokes, and relief washes over me when the bill is paid.

The car ride home is silent. This happens with Brian, of course. He's either thinking of work or thinking of how to carefully curate his feedback on the evening. Either way, I find comfort in the silence. The glow of passing streetlights flickers across his face, highlighting the sharp lines of his jaw, the set of his mouth. His jacket is draped over the backseat, the scent of his cologne thick in the small, enclosed space.

I stare out the window, watching the suburban town blur past, my fingers twisting the fabric of my dress in my lap. The car is too quiet. Or maybe it's just me, hyper-aware of the way my pulse thrums beneath my skin, a reminder of the way my heart still hasn't settled since I left Albany.

Brian's voice cuts through the silence.

"So, how was your set?"

My stomach clenches.

I blink, forcing myself to inhale as if that will somehow clear my mind, steady my heartbeat. I should've seen this question coming. Because in Brian's mind, I was in Albany today for a gig—not for Hunter. Not for some long, meandering walk through streets soaked in nostalgia. Not for a kiss I shouldn't have let happen but can't stop replaying.

I exhale. Lie.

"I bombed."

Brian clicks his tongue, shaking his head. "Ah, you must've done that rabbit joke."

I don't respond. But he does. He glances at me briefly, like he's already figured it out. "Char, I told you that joke wasn't appropriate for a female comedian."

A sharp inhale. A lump forms in my throat. The set may have been a lie but that joke is quintessential to my work. It's why I'm being booked in the first place. Over 3 million views on YouTube and thousands of comments. Worse?

Just a few hours ago, that joke was brilliant. Just a few hours ago, I was standing in the street, eyes locked with Hunter's when he said that stand-up suits me.

But now, I sit in the passenger seat of my own life, watching Brian's hands grip the steering wheel, watching the world pass by as he effortlessly dismantles the one thing that makes me feel like me.

That feeling birds back in. The quiet, suffocating weight of it. That itch beneath my skin. That slow, sinking realization that no matter how much I tell myself this is the right path, I can't ignore the way my stomach tightens when he speaks.

The way my pulse thrums with the knowledge that Hunter heard me—Brian corrects me. I swallow sharply, forcing the words down like a bitter pill.

Brian flicks on his turn signal, shooting me a quick glance. "You okay?"

His voice is steady. Earnest. And for a second, I feel something close to guilt. Because he loves me, doesn't he? He's steady. Dependable. He wants to build a life with me.

He chose me.

I nod, adjusting my posture, smoothing my dress over my legs. "Of course. It was just a long drive." It's not the time to go in on how his one statement is unraveling my entire existence.

I press my palm against my thigh, focusing on the weight of it, the feeling of something solid beneath my fingertips. But the lump in my throat remains.

And no matter how much I try to shake it—I can't ignore the truth.

I may have bombed tonight.

But not on stage.

Chapter Six *For weeks later.*

The house is buzzing with energy.

There's music playing—something soft and orchestral, the kind of instrumental melody you'd expect to underscore the opening of a wedding montage. It's all perfectly curated, like everything else today. The scent of peonies and Chanel perfume lingers in the air, mingling with the faintest trace of hairspray as the makeup artist floats between women, sweeping powder over Effie's cheekbones and pinning the last twist of my mother's hair into place.

Effie is in full PR mode—poised, efficient, holding a mimosa in one hand and her phone in the other like both are extensions of her body. She's been saying for years that she'll be my publicist when my comedy career inevitably takes off. "You're one viral set away from being the next Chelsea Handler," she's always said. Today, she's the reason Vogue picked up our wedding for their *Small Love Stories* feature. Apparently, the "North Shore debutante marries hedge fund darling while quietly chasing stand-up dreams" angle sells. She's right, of course. She always is.

"Photographer's on schedule," she says, not looking up. "The florist delivered the bouquets—white roses, no red streaks. We are not doing a Valentine's Day horror show. Brian's en route to the church, and I told the caterer no raw bar because we are not letting you smell like oysters all day."

I manage a laugh. "You're a saint."

"I know," she says breezily, popping a strawberry into her mouth before pivoting toward my mother. "And, Mrs. Carmichael, the guest book will be up front so your cousins don't have another full meltdown like they did at your niece's wedding."

My mom dabs the corner of her eye with a tissue, her silk champagne gown catching the morning light. "What would we do without you, Effie?"

"Crash and burn," she says, and winks at me in the mirror.

Franny won't leave my side. She's curled against my leg, eyes big and warm and knowing. Every time I shift, she shifts. She knows something's off, even if no one else does. I tell myself it's just nerves. Butterflies. Cold feet. Totally normal.

But it doesn't feel normal.

The makeup artist applies my final coat of lipstick, and my hands tremble. Just enough for Effie to notice. Just enough for her expression to flicker—briefly—before she smooths it away.

This morning should feel like magic. It should be joy and tears and champagne and laughter. And for a while, it was. I was happy. Nervous—but happy. I watched my mom cry and felt so full. I watched Effie run around like a one-woman army and felt lucky to be loved like this. I am lucky. This is a six-figure wedding. My life is beautiful. My future is secure.

And still—That pressure behind my ribs. That weight that won't move.

After the dinner with Brian's bosses, I almost ended everything. Not because of Hunter—though kissing him was the ignition—but because of Brian's comment. About my joke. The joke that built my following. The joke that made me feel seen. He dismissed it like it was something beneath me. Something inappropriate.

I stayed quiet for two days after. Said nothing beyond the basics. Then I spent a night in the city with Effie and Franny, crashing on her couch with takeout and wine. I told her everything. The kiss. The confusion. The guilt.

And in typical Effie fashion, she said exactly what I needed to hear.

"It's not worth it, Char."

She was right. One kiss, one bad comment—none of it should unravel a life we've built. So I went home. I walked up the porch steps still unsure of what I'd say. But waiting inside were thousands of peonies and roses, their scent thick in the air. A trail of petals led to the kitchen, where a box sat on the island with a note:

I was a jerk about your joke. I'm sure not everyone agreed with Robin about dressing in drag. Please accept my apology. I love you, B.

Inside the box was a first-edition *Mrs. Doubtfire* poster, signed by the entire cast. My breath caught in my throat.

We're not perfect. But we're trying.

So I said yes again. Silently. Internally. Resolutely. I promised myself I would move forward. That I would show up today and mean it.

The gown is stunning—satin, sculpted bodice, lace sleeves. It feels classic. The kind of dress a woman chooses when she knows exactly where she's going. My mother clasps a delicate diamond bracelet around my wrist, her hands gentle, reverent. "You look perfect," she whispers, blinking back tears.

I smile. I squeeze her fingers. I let her believe I feel it too.

Outside, the florist is arranging bouquets into tall vases, the photographer moving around me in a blur, snapping shots of ribbons and rings and details I'll forget by tomorrow. Effie's voice floats in from the hallway, corralling vendors, confirming timelines.

She steps back into the room just as I'm adjusting my veil. She stops short, her gaze softening.

"Effie?" I ask.

Her throat bobs. Then she grins. "Jesus. You're actually getting married."

I laugh. A real one. But something flickers inside me—uncertain and hollow. I don't have time to name it. The moment moves on. Effie shifts back into gear.

"Let's get you outside for portraits before the car gets here. I've got your emergency bag, your vows, your phone—everything. All you have to do is smile."

We're in the front yard now, and the golden morning light catches every shimmer on my dress. The photographer directs me to tilt my chin, soften my eyes, turn slightly. Effie watches from the driveway, my phone clutched in one hand, scrolling with the other.

Then—
A ping.

Effie glances down. Her fingers go still. Her eyes widen, lips parting just slightly.

I shift, sensing the change. "Everything okay?"

She snaps out of it, too quick to be natural. "Yeah. Dog walker confirmed for this afternoon."

I nod, turning back to the camera, angling my bouquet just so. I don't see her lift my phone. Don't see her read the message again.

Hunter: *I still love you. Please don't marry him.*

She stares. Just for a breath. Then—
Delete.

The message disappears.

Effie moves with precision, gathering bags, directing people toward the car. Her voice is calm, steady. "Alright, let's go! We don't keep grooms waiting."

Franny barks once as I step toward the open door of the car, almost like she's trying to tell me something. Effie squeezes my hand before I climb in, nails digging into my palm.

She doesn't say a word.

Because she knows what I don't need to know.

The door closes. The engine hums to life.

Outside, the world continues. Beautiful and blurred.
Inside, I sit perfectly still, hands folded in my lap, a bride on her way to her wedding. To a man who loves me. To a future I chose. One that looks like everything I ever said I wanted.

And somewhere—miles away—Hunter Maisley stands alone.

Phone still in his hand.
Thumb still hovering.
The words gone, but the ache still sharp.

The world keeps spinning.
But in his chest, time has stopped.

Chapter Seven - *Hunter*

The air in Buffalo is too still. The kind of stillness that gets under your skin. The sky is a pale, indecisive blue—washed-out and exhausted. I sit at the kitchen table, hunched over a cold cup of coffee, and for the first time in weeks, I can't pretend everything is fine.

Charlotte is getting married today.

I shouldn't know that. Shouldn't have it marked in my head like it's a national holiday. But I've known this date for months. I've counted down to it in a way I haven't counted anything since college. Every day since I kissed her, I've thought about reaching out. Every day, I've stared at my phone and told myself: not yet. Wait. Maybe she'll call it off. If she was going to, I'd know. There'd be signs. A change in her tone online. A post taken down. Something. Anything. But the days passed and she said nothing. She gave me nothing.

Still, I waited. Because the alternative—that she was really going through with it—was too much to sit with.

Kelly is still asleep in our bed upstairs. We haven't touched each other in weeks. We barely speak unless it's about groceries or bills or something mundane like who left the back light on. The silence between us has stretched so long it's become its own language.

I've tried to be better. Tried to show up. But it's like I've been living in a fog since Albany. Like I left the best version of myself in the middle of that street when Charlotte walked away.

Three nights ago, I woke up drenched in sweat. Same dream I always have—her hand in mine, her laugh echoing in my ears, her body curved into mine like we were made for it. And then—her face when she caught me with Fiona. That expression. That devastation. It guts me every time. Not because I forgot what I did. But because I'll never forget what I lost.

When I wake up from those dreams, I don't cry. I just lie there, staring at the ceiling, letting the weight of my own decisions crush me. And this morning, I did the thing I swore I wouldn't do.

I picked up my phone. I typed the words: "I still love you. Please don't marry him."

And then I hit send.

There was no thinking. Just instinct. Just desperation.

I flipped the phone back over and stared at the grain of the table like I could will myself into a different reality.

Nothing came. Not even a read receipt. So I opened Instagram. I didn't hesitate. Searched her handle, the one I still know by heart. Charlotte Carmichael.

Her profile is still public. Still full of stand-up clips and blurry late-night food pics. Posts that feel like private jokes I don't get to be part of anymore. I scrolled. Past engagement shots. Past the wedding countdown. Past her dress fitting. And then I saw it.

A boomerang in the back of a car. Champagne. Effie next to her. Big smiles. The caption: "Next stop: forever."

That's when it hit me. She saw the message—and still got in the car.

It's not like I thought one text would change her mind. I'm not that delusional. But somewhere in me—in the part that still believes in miracles—I hoped.

I grabbed the bottle of scotch from the top shelf. The good stuff, the one Kelly got me for my birthday last year. I poured a glass. Then another. And another.

I drank until the day turned blurry. Until the ache in my chest dulled just enough to breathe. Until I could stop picturing her in that dress.

The bottle was half gone by the time the notification came in.

A new post.

A black-and-white photo. Candles. Laughter in a blur. The caption: "Married."

One word. Final. Brutal.

It's done. I've lost her. Not just in theory. Not just in a daydream. For real.

I sat there, blinking through the alcohol haze, trying to convince myself I didn't care. Trying to pretend that I hadn't gambled everything and lost. Again.

The front door opened around seven. Keys jingled. Kelly's heels clicked against the floor.

"Jesus Christ, Hunter," she said, the second she stepped into the kitchen. "Are you drunk?"

I didn't answer. Just stared into my glass like the bottom would reveal something useful.

She tossed her bag on the counter and crossed her arms. "It's Saturday. We were supposed to meet my parents. You knew that."

I blinked up at her, slow and stupid. "Forgot."

"Forgot?" Her voice sharpened, slicing through the room. "You've been checked out for weeks. Months, maybe. What the hell is going on with you?"

I didn't know how to answer that. Or maybe I did —I just didn't have the guts to say it.

That I'm in love with someone else. That I fucked up the only thing that ever felt real. That I've been living in the past because the present is unbearable.

Instead, I reached for the bottle and poured another drink.

"Unbelievable," she muttered, spinning on her heel. "You know what? Stay here. Drink yourself into oblivion. Whatever. I'm done."

The door slammed.

I sat in the silence that followed, the scotch burning down my throat, the weight in my chest heavier than ever.

I had seven years to be the man Charlotte deserved.

Instead, I let her marry someone else.

And now, I have to live with that.

Chapter Eight - *Seven Years Later*

The text comes in at 5:42 PM.

I'm sitting cross-legged on the couch in the green room, flipping through my set list while Franny snores softly at my feet, her warm, familiar body pressed against mine like a weighted blanket. Her presence is grounding—something solid in the chaos of pre-show adrenaline and fluorescent lighting.

It's been three months since the start of my now-sold-out "This Is Chaotic" tour. Effie, true to her word and then some, has become my PR team, tour manager, crisis negotiator, and the right half of my brain. After our wedding got picked up by *Vogue*, interest in my YouTube channel exploded. Suddenly I was everywhere—booked and busy, performing on late-night shows with my cleanest material, fielding movie cameos, roasting Kim Kardashian on national television. Effie launched a podcast for me—*Everything Chaotic*—a once-a-week ramble that somehow managed to rack up over three million downloads in its first year. And by the end of that year, she formed *Chaos Industries* to keep track of the whirlwind. The podcast alone was making more than Brian ever did, which was... ironic, considering the man had built his identity around his LinkedIn profile.

And now, I'm a well-known—okay, famous—comedienne. With a tour bus, a glam team, a manager who negotiates my streaming rights, and fans who show up in full sequin to mimic my look. It's a dream. But it's exhausting. So when my phone buzzes beside me, I expect it to be Effie checking in, Eddie sending a contract update, or maybe someone from the press needing a quote. Instead, it's a number I don't recognize.

516: My name is Cara. I'm so sorry. Thought you should know.

My brow furrows. My thumb hovers. I know better—I *do*—but I open the message anyway.

And everything tilts.

The first image is unmistakably Brian. Naked. In bed. With someone who is very much not me.

The second is worse—their mouths tangled together, his hand in her hair. The third has him curled around her like muscle memory, like how he used to hold me when we were still good. Or at least, when I thought we were.

Beneath the images, her message reads:

Cara: I didn't know he was married at first. But now I do. And he's married to you, which is worse. I love your comedy.

I go completely still. My vision narrows, the air turns thick, and the static in my brain overtakes every coherent thought. I can't breathe. I can't move. Franny stirs beneath me, lifting her head like she knows something's wrong—because something *is* wrong. Everything is.

The door swings open.

Effie strides in, mid-sentence. "Alright, pre-show checklist—press is handled, your agent's here, and Eddie—"

She freezes.

"Charlotte?"

I don't answer. Can't.

She steps closer, all business now forgotten. Her clipboard hangs at her side. "What happened?"

I turn the screen toward her with slow, numb fingers. She takes the phone from my hand and reads. I watch her face harden, her jaw lock in place, the rage blooming behind her eyes like something she's keeping barely restrained.

"This motherfucker," she hisses, voice like cut glass.

I still haven't spoken. I've gone completely offline. The woman inside me—the one who tells jokes, writes bits, commands audiences of twelve thousand—is nowhere to be found.

Brian. My husband. The man who cheered me on, even when he didn't quite understand what I was doing. Who sent flowers backstage, left me notes in my script margins. Who walked beside me through magazine spreads and after-parties and red carpets. Who played the role of partner so perfectly, I forgot it might just be that: a role.

And now there's Cara. Bold enough to text me. Bold enough to include photos.

Effie's still holding my phone when Eddie walks in. After my first comedy special blew up, I pulled him onto my team. He's all numbers, logistics, and negotiations—exactly what I needed to survive the machine of success. He's my older brother by seven years, sharp and unapologetically protective. We're not the "I love you" kind of siblings. But I trust him like gravity.

He takes one look at the two of us and doesn't miss a beat. "What's going on?"

Effie hands him the phone. "Brian's been cheating. Her name's Cara."

Eddie reads, and his whole demeanor shifts. "You're fucking kidding me."

I let out a sound somewhere between a laugh and a gasp. Eddie never liked Brian. He warned me once, maybe twice, to reconsider marrying someone who didn't know how to handle my shine. Between him and Hunter, maybe I should've listened. But I can't unravel the past. Not right now.

Eddie rakes a hand through his hair, already moving. "Tell me you have a prenup."

Effie cuts in. "No prenup. He had the upper hand financially back then. But everything tied to Charlotte is under *Chaos Industries*. The LLC is safe."

Eddie nods. "Good. Then I'll take care of it. You don't worry about a thing."

I stand and hug him. It's brief but loaded with all the things we don't say out loud. I'm grateful for him in a way that has nothing to do with blood and everything to do with loyalty.

Effie wraps her arms around both of us. "You're going to survive this. And when you do, you're going to make it gold. You always do."

I manage a breath. Then a half-smile. "Guess I just found new material."

The Fox Theater is electric. The energy in the room is thick—buzzing, alive, almost sticky with anticipation. I stand side stage as my opener warms up the crowd, watching women file in dressed in their best disco outfits—sequins, bell-bottoms, feathered hair—in full homage to my brand. Every time, it knocks the wind out of me a little. This is *my* life. After all the nights in basement clubs and joke-writing marathons and nerves so bad I thought I might pass out—this is what it's led to. And it's been hard. But it's been worth it.

Effie appears at my side, her clipboard tucked under her arm, chewing a piece of gum like it personally wronged her.

"How are you feeling?" she asks.

"I forgot about the text for the last ten minutes," I say. "Does that make me a sociopath?"

"No, babe. It makes you a fucking boss babe."

I cringe—because I *hate* that term—but I know Effie means it with love. And besides, she's not wrong.

"I'm going to talk about this in the set," I say. "And when it gets out, he's going to lose his goddamn mind."

"Who fucking cares? It's your story to tell. Your honesty is why there are thousands of women out there in shiny outfits waiting to scream for you. Just maybe don't use her real name, you know? Defamation and all that."

The lights flicker, the two-minute warning. The announcer's voice booms over the speakers, listing off the usual theater etiquette—no phones, don't leave unless you're dying, yada yada.

"Ladies and gentlemen," the voice crescendos, "please welcome to the stage... your favorite disco-loving comedienne, Charlotte Carmichael!"

Effie smacks my butt, and I smirk over my shoulder as I step out into the light.

The second my foot hits the stage, the crowd erupts. It's a wall of sound. For one suspended moment, I forget how much I want to fall apart.

I grip the mic and let the applause settle.

"Let's talk about men."

Laughter rolls through the theater—low, warm, expectant.

I tilt my head, stretching out the silence just enough. "Ever notice how men *cannot* handle being sick?"

More laughter. Nods. A woman near the front pumps her fist.

"A migraine?" I scoff. "Suddenly it's a full Shakespearean production. Act One: Moaning on the couch. Act Two: Whispering, 'I don't think I'm gonna make it.' Act Three: Googling *early signs of a brain aneurysm.*"

The crowd leans in, already hooked.

"My husband—bless him—gets migraines all the time. And wouldn't you know it, they always hit around five o'clock. Just as he's about to leave the office. That's when I get the text: 'Hey babe, a migraine just hit. I can't drive. Gonna wait it out 'til the medicine kicks in.'"

Scattered giggles, eyes narrowing with curiosity.

"Well, tonight I learned something new about migraines," I say. "Apparently, they can have specific names depending on where they hit."

A beat.

"My husband's migraine is named *Cassandra*. And she happens to hit below the waist."

Gasps. Laughter. Someone yells "OH NO" from the mezzanine.

"Yeah. About an hour ago—*one* hour ago—I found out my husband is having an affair."

I mime scrolling on my phone, eyes wide. "She sent me photos, y'all. Not subtle hints. Not a cryptic DM. *Photos.* Like she was auditioning for *CSI: Homewrecker Unit.*"

Laughter builds, rolling in waves.

I pull the mic from the stand and start to pace the stage. The adrenaline has kicked in now. I'm warm. Sharp. Dangerous.

"And I haven't even confronted him yet."

Gasps turn into gleeful oooooohs.

"Yeah. You guys are the first people I'm talking to about this. You ever have 12,000 people emotionally prepare you to ruin a man's life?"

The crowd loses it.

"I mean, I'm still deciding how I want to handle it. Do I go calm? Therapist voice? You know the one. The kind that already *knows* the answer but waits for you to say it?"

I cross my arms, tilt my head, and drop my voice to a deadpan whisper.

"Brian. Is there something... you'd like to tell me?"

The audience roars.

"Or do I come in hot? Like *Cops* finale energy? Just kick in the door like, 'WHERE'S CASSANDRA?!'"

I widen my eyes and form a finger gun, scanning the audience like I'm about to tackle a suspect. The laughter doubles.

"Or—do I go full mind game? Just sit across from him at dinner and start humming the theme from *Law & Order*."

I hum the iconic dun-dun! with perfect timing.

The crowd explodes. Someone's wheezing.

I shake my head, still pacing.

"But what really gets me," I say, "is the *audacity* of this man."

Everyone quiets slightly, sensing a twist coming.

"I'm on tour. My last show is tomorrow in Albany. He won't see me for three more days. And when I finally get home, I *guarantee* he's going to look up from his PlayStation and say—"

I pause, shift my weight, drop my voice.

"'What's wrong, babe?'"

The crowd is already giggling.

"Scratching his balls. The same ones *Cassandra* was probably licking while I was gone."

I mime it—big, exaggerated, center stage.

Laughter erupts. Someone stands to clap.

"And when I tell him I *know*, he's going to give me this look."

I walk to the front of the stage, mouth slack, eyes blank—like a golden retriever who just got caught eating drywall.

The laughter swells again.

"And then—then!—he'll hit me with the classic line: 'It didn't mean anything.'"

I blink. Stare. Let it land.

Then I throw one arm in the air.

"IT. DIDN'T. MEAN. ANYTHING?!"

The roar is instant.

I lean into the mic, dropping my voice low again. "Sir. You risked half your retirement savings, my emotional stability, and the *sanctity of my dog's happiness*... for something that didn't mean anything?"

People are crying-laughing now.

"Oh, but it gets worse." I lift a finger. "You wanna know what *Cassandra* said in the text? This is real—she said, 'I just wanted to come to you... as a woman.'"

Groans ripple across the theater.

"Ladies," I say, raising both hands, "if you *ever* find yourself typing those words? Stop. Delete the message. Close the app. And throw your phone into the nearest body of water."

It's chaos. Pure, brilliant chaos. I feel it in my chest—the high of being heard. Of turning hurt into power.

"But hey," I say, softer now. "Maybe this is all my fault. Maybe I should've seen the signs."

I tap my chin, pretending to ponder.

"You know how I should've known he was cheating?" I squint at the crowd, hold up one finger.

"Because men... do not take showers before going to the gym."

The room *erupts*.

"Ladies, I'm telling you—if your man suddenly starts getting *too* clean, too well-dressed, and *too* enthusiastic about spin class? He's not going for cardio. He's going for *Cassandra*."

Screams. Applause. Phones raised. Women slapping their thighs.

I let the moment hang, and then lower my voice.

"But for real—I know what you're going to say. 'Oh, Charlotte, everything happens for a reason.'"

I shake my head slowly.

"No. Sometimes things just happen... because your husband is a piece of shit."

The crowd *erupts*. Standing ovation. Applause crashing over the stage like waves. I place a hand over my heart, grinning through the sweat and adrenaline and heartbreak.

"Thank you, Fox Theater! You've been amazing!"

I drop the mic into the stand and walk off stage, the lights dimming behind me, the sound of the crowd echoing like a heartbeat.

And for just one moment—I don't feel broken anymore.

Three hours and one overly handsy meet-and-greet later, I'm back at the hotel, collapsing face-first onto the bed. I kick off my heels and let out a breath so deep it feels like I've been holding it for seven years.

The show was electric. Maybe the best of my career. And now, as the adrenaline drains from my body, all that's left is the quiet thud of exhaustion.

Franny jumps up beside me, curling into my side like she's been waiting all night for this moment. My little road dog—eight years older and still more loyal than any man I've ever known.

Across the room, Effie is scrolling on her phone, feet tucked beneath her like she owns the place. "We posted the divorce announcement on Instagram while you were on stage," she says casually. "Didn't seem worth giving him time to spin the narrative. Eddie says ticket sales jumped twenty percent."

I close my eyes. "Perfect. My heartbreak is now a business model."

Effie looks over at me. "You okay?"

I laugh—dry and hollow. "Oh, totally. Just another night turning personal devastation into content."

She doesn't laugh. Because she knows me. She knows when the jokes are armor.

I stare up at the ceiling, words bubbling up before I can stop them. "I keep thinking about karma."

She tilts her head. "Why?"

"I don't know." I shift slightly, Franny resettling beside me. "Maybe this is the universe settling the score. For kissing Hunter. Back in Albany. Before the wedding."

Effie doesn't even blink. "That is the dumbest thing you've ever said."

The words land with a clean, sharp snap. No room for argument. No space for guilt.

I nod once, absorbing it. She's right.

Tomorrow I fly to Albany—the final stop of the tour. It had felt poetic, once. I did my first stand-up set there in college. A full-circle kind of ending.

But now it feels less like poetry and more like a setup. Like a loop I never quite escaped.

I kissed a man in Albany before I got married.

Now, I'm going back. Unmarried. Unraveled.

And something tells me I'm about to face more than just a homecoming.

Chapter Nine

Albany still feels like her—the girl I used to be.

I don't know why I thought it would feel different now. All these years later, a world away from the version of me who once walked these streets in worn-out boots and oversized scarves, always halfway between heartbreak and ambition. But the moment I step off that plane at 4:30 a.m., I feel her. Like she never left.

The girl who stayed up late writing jokes no one would hear. Who kissed the wrong person in the wrong parking lot. Who thought a stable relationship might be the answer to the chaos in her brain.

That girl is still here, haunting the corners of this city like she's waiting for me to notice.

And now? I have everything she wanted.

A name people know. A sold-out tour. Viral reels. A contract with Netflix and a podcast empire built off the back of my chaos. But I don't have a home

—not the kind that feels permanent. Not the kind that isn't at risk of crumbling with the next betrayal.

I tell myself it's fine. That some people just aren't built for marriage. That I'm simply a product of my parents—two beautiful disasters who looked great on paper and awful in person. But even knowing that, it still stings.

After check-in, I don't bother unpacking. I just grab Franny's leash and decide to walk it out. The benefit of flying private—courtesy of a corporate sponsorship Effie somehow finessed while half-asleep—is that Franny can go wherever I go. Emotional support status: earned.

The air is crisp, just on the edge of winter. One of those mornings that smells like frost and new beginnings. Franny trots ahead like she's on a mission. Seven years in, and she still greets every walk like it's opening night.

My life is a category five dumpster fire, but at least I've got her.

She veers toward a pile of leaves, tail wagging like she just found enlightenment in the form of old garbage.

"You've got no idea how lucky you are," I mutter, giving the leash a soft tug. "No taxes. No heartbreak. No complicated texts from women named Cara. You roll in trash, people call you quirky. I do it, I need therapy."

She sneezes in response. Unbothered. Regal.

We keep moving. The streets are quiet, and I let the stillness settle in my chest like a sedative. The early morning hush before the world wakes up. Before I have to be *on* again.

Franny stops to sniff a rusted metal post.

I look up.

The parking garage.

My breath catches in my throat.

It's the same one. Seven years ago. The night before I got married. The place where I kissed

Hunter Maisley like my soul had short-circuited and my mouth was the only way to reset.

I remember the cold. The sharp wind biting at my cheeks. The heat of his hands on my waist. The way my fingers curled into his coat like I could anchor myself to him and everything would stop spinning.

It wasn't just a kiss.

It was a confession. A dare. A question I never had the courage to answer.

And then I pulled away. Got in my car. Drove back to Brian like nothing had happened.

I chose Brian.

I chose safety. And now, standing here with Franny beside me and divorce papers on the horizon, I can't help but wonder if I ever really made the right call.

I grip the leash tighter. Enough. The past has teeth, and I've let it bite too many times.

We head back to the hotel.

The room is too clean. Hotel-clean. The kind that smells like lemon-scented professionalism and no actual life. I toss my hoodie onto the accent chair, climb into bed, and feel Franny curl up against me like she's trying to hold the pieces together.

My phone buzzes on the nightstand.

Brian.

I ignore it. It buzzes again. I flip it face-down.

Silence.

Then— A knock.

My stomach drops.

Franny lifts her head, ears twitching. No tail wag. No joyful leap off the bed.

Just stillness. A second knock. Followed by his voice.

"Char. Please."

My name in his voice sounds like static—familiar, worn down, desperate.

I get up slowly, like every step requires its own negotiation. Walk to the door. Unlock it.

And there he is.

Brian. My husband. Or what's left of him.

His hair is uncombed. His dress shirt is crumpled like he's been sleeping in it. The tie around his neck is half-loosened, like it's been choking him all day. His face is drawn, eyes hollowed out by guilt or exhaustion or the dawning realization that he doesn't get to control the narrative anymore.

But it's the look that gets me—the one that used to work. The one that used to say, *I'm sorry, I love you, I'll do better.*

And for a long time, I believed it.

But now?

I don't know that I do anymore.

"I fucked up," he says, voice hoarse—like he's barely slept, like he's been practicing this line the entire drive from Long Island, mouthing it to his rearview mirror the whole way up the Thruway.

I lean against the doorframe, arms crossed. Steady. Cold. Holding the line.

"That's an understatement."

Brian exhales, sharp and shaky. "I—Christ, Char, I don't even know where to start. I was stupid. I was selfish. But I swear to God, she meant nothing."

I let out a laugh—dry, hollow. "Amazing. Do you guys all get the same manual? Page one: *Tell her it didn't mean anything.*"

He takes a step closer. Desperate. Like proximity might help.

"I love you."

I don't flinch.

"I love you," he says again, more urgent this time, like repetition might wipe the slate clean.

Beside me, Franny lets out a low, unimpressed huff. She shifts her weight until she's pressed firmly against my leg—guardian mode activated.

Even the dog isn't buying this shit.

Brian notices. "Come on, Franny. Not even you?"

Franny stares at him like she's ready to call her own lawyer.

I fold my arms tighter.

"Char, please," Brian says. "You don't have to forgive me. I just—I need to talk to you."

Before I can respond, the door next to me swings open. Effie.

Because of course we have conjoining rooms.

She steps out in sweatpants, an "EAT THE RICH" t-shirt, and a half-dried face mask smeared across her forehead like war paint. She takes one look at

Brian and narrows her eyes, like she's assessing whether or not she should mace him.

"Nope," she says. "No. Not happening."

Brian opens his mouth, but Effie cuts in, stepping directly in front of me like a tiny, furious bouncer.

"I don't care what you have to say," she continues. "I don't care if you wrote a TED Talk about your feelings. You need to leave."

"I just want to talk to my wife," Brian pleads, his voice cracking.

"She doesn't want to talk to you."

"I can speak for myself," I mutter.

Effie shoots me a look. I shrug. "She's not wrong."

Brian looks between us, clearly calculating which words might still save him. He settles on a classic.

"This isn't fair."

Effie lets out a bark of laughter. "Oh, I'm *sorry*— are *you* feeling unfairly treated? Because if we're throwing around the word *fair*, I'd love to pull up those photos again. Maybe put them in a slideshow? Set it to Sarah McLachlan?"

His jaw tightens. His eyes land back on me, soft and pleading.

And then something in me cracks.

"You want to talk? Fine," I snap. "Let's talk. You humiliated me."

I step forward, words like a match to dry kindling.

"I know this wasn't perfect. I know my travel schedule was insane. I know I've been gone more than I've been home. I carry that guilt. Every day. But I stayed loyal. I believed in us. I trusted you."

I pause, letting the words hang. Then I drop the hammer.

"And you still chose to throw it away for some basic bitch in a tan bra."

Silence.

"You didn't just cheat on me—you put me at risk. You risked *everything*—my health, my reputation, our life—for what? A quick fuck and a selfie? This isn't some mistake we work through over brunch. This is *unforgivable*."

His face crumples.

"There's nothing left to say, Brian. We could sit here and dissect a thousand what-ifs, but it won't change this. You burned it to the ground."

I take one step back.

"You'll hear from my lawyer."

And then I close the door.

It clicks shut, final and sure.

For a moment, I just stand there, hand still on the knob, breath catching in my throat.

Behind me, Franny hops back on the bed and curls up like nothing happened. Like the world didn't just tilt on its axis. Like she's still safe in her version of things.

I let out a breath. Long. Measured.

Effie watches me from the edge of the bed, her expression unreadable. Then, carefully:

"You okay?" I nod once. She tilts her head. "You wanna go get brunch?"

A beat. Then I laugh—really laugh, for the first time in what feels like forever.

"God, yes."

Chapter Ten

The Egg feels different now.

I stand center stage during mic check, rolling my shoulders, adjusting the mic stand. The crew moves around me—fixing lights, running cables, shouting checks into headsets like we're launching a rocket instead of telling jokes.

Seven years ago, I was performing for drink tickets in half-empty bars. Fighting for five minutes of stage time sandwiched between amateur improv troupes and dudes who thought saying "vagina" loudly into a mic was edgy comedy.

Now? I've done the circuit.
Sold out Chicago. Got bumped up at The Comedy Store. Been interviewed by Fallon, profiled in *Vulture*, and recognized—more than once—at LAX by women in airport Crocs who whisper "Are you... her?" like they've spotted a unicorn in a baseball cap.

I've played bigger venues. L.A. clubs. Vegas residencies. Theater tours that stretched across countries and time zones. But this?

This is home.

Albany has a way of sinking into my bones, even after all these years. I spent college running away from my past. And now?

Now I'm running toward it.

Offstage, Effie paces, clipboard in hand, barking into her headset.

"Who the hell put the bottled water backstage right instead of left? Do you want Charlotte to trip over it mid-set? I swear to God, one of you is getting fired, and it's not me—"

I snort, adjusting the mic.
"Effie, relax. I don't need a union rep over a Dasani."

She shoots me a glare, but I catch the smirk.

"I'm just saying, if you eat shit on stage because of a rogue water bottle, I'm not dragging your ass off."

"Damn. Fourteen years of friendship, and *that's* where you draw the line?"

Before she can fire back, there's a commotion backstage.

I glance over—and oh, Jesus Christ.

My parents.

Somehow, my divorced, bickering, permanently exasperating parents have made the drive from Long Island without killing each other, and now they're here. Great.

My mom sees me first and, in an instant, I'm enveloped in a Chanel-scented death grip.

"My baby," she croons, clutching me like I've just returned from war. "Oh my God. Are you okay? Why didn't you *call* me about your divorce? You look thin. Are you eating? You're not eating."

"Mom. Please. For the love of God—"

My dad claps me on the back. "Gonna be a hell of a show, kiddo."

My mom swats him. "The show isn't the *only* thing going on, Anthony. Show some support. She doesn't need your pressure."

"Pressure?" he scoffs. "This one thrives under pressure. You should've seen her at six years old doing a tight five at Aunt Maria's wedding—had the whole table in tears."

I pinch the bridge of my nose.

Inviting my parents felt like a good idea before my life imploded less than twenty-four hours ago. Now—with Brian's surprise visit, the weight of the tour's end, and the full-body exhaustion of keeping it together—it feels like a deeply unwise decision.

"Yes, I should've called about the divorce. It happened yesterday. I knew I'd see you tonight. I love you both. Please leave before I walk into traffic."

Effie slides in like a gift from the gods. Hands on their backs, steering them away with the ease of a professional hostage negotiator.

"Okay, Mr. and Mrs. Carmichael—there's free wine in the green room. Please, for all our sakes, enjoy it."

I exhale.

I love them. I really do.

But I have a show to do.

The lights are blinding, but I've learned to find the audience anyway. You feel them before you see them. That ripple of energy. That breath before the applause.

And then it hits.

Thunderous. Rolling through The Egg like a wave.

I stand there, mic in hand, letting it wash over me. I still feel the rush like it's the first time. Every. Single. Time.

Then, I lean into the mic.

"You ever realize you hit a certain age where you can't just... do things anymore? Like, the other day, I sat down too fast, and my spine whispered, 'That's it. We had a good run.'"

Laughter. A few claps.

I smirk.

"No, seriously. I sneezed last week and now I have a *permanent injury*. My doctor called it a 'muscle spasm.' No, sir. This is the moment my body said, 'We're done now.'"

More laughter. Someone whistles from the balcony.

"And don't get me started on metabolism. Remember when we were younger? You could eat an entire pizza at 2 a.m. and be fine? I eat one breadstick now and my jeans are like, *you thought*."

The crowd roars. I pace the stage, riding it.

"I was at a bar the other night, right? Guy asks me, 'Hey, what's your sign?' I said, 'Mostly exhausted.'"

Beat.

"He says, 'No, really, what's your sign?' I said, 'The one outside that says Exit.'"

The laughter doubles. I give it space, then pivot.

"But okay, let's be real. I know why you're here."

A beat. A perfectly timed pause.

"You want to hear about the headline news... I mean, I can't believe Bennifer broke up again. What is that now—season four?"

The room erupts—woots, groans, applause, the sound of collective judgment and devotion to pop culture.

I sigh, resting a hand on my hip.

"Yeah, yeah. Hollywood's favorite couple's relationship crumbled, and so did mine. The only difference is I didn't have a yacht in the Amalfi. I have a dog named Franny, a tour bus, and a husband who couldn't keep it in his pants."

Laughter—sharp, loud, a little unhinged.

"But sure, let's talk divorce. One minute you're in a white dress making promises, and the next, you're explaining to a judge why your ex doesn't deserve the house, the dog, or, frankly, oxygen."

Laughter. Real laughter. That generous, rowdy kind that vibrates in your chest.

I scan the crowd. The faces. The glow of phones.

And then—
I see him.

Hunter.

Sitting in the audience.

I freeze. Just a second. Just a flicker. But my heart slams against my ribs so hard, I swear the mic picks it up.

He's watching me. Of course he is. Everyone is. But he's different. He always has been.

I force a smirk, flick my eyes back to the crowd, and shove it down. All of it. On the spot, I pivot the set.

"You ever see someone from your past and think, *Damn, I should've sued for emotional damages*?"

The audience howls. I hold up a hand, milking it.

"No, seriously. Why don't we have small claims court for exes? I shouldn't have to Venmo request you for the years you shaved off my life. There should be a judge. A jury of my peers. A full-on trial."

I'm flying now. The rhythm clicks into place. I forget the nerves. I forget everything except the feeling.

For the next hour, I crush it.

The migraine named Cassandra bit lands even harder than last night.

And I close it all out with a nod to the beginning.

"And just like that—my rabbit is back in rotation. Thank you, Albany," I say, pressing a hand to my chest. "You've been amazing."

The lights dim.

The sound swells, then swallows me whole.

And just like that—

It's over.

I turn from the crowd, heart pounding in my ears, feet moving before my mind catches up.

Because I know what's waiting for me.

Not just the high. Not just the after-party. Not just my parents.

A ghost from my past is here.

Hunter is here.

And no matter how far I've come, a part of me is still standing in that parking garage seven years ago, waiting for him to catch up.

Chapter Eleven

The moment I step off stage, I'm hit with a wall of voices, cheers, and limbs pulling me into Chanel-scented hugs and cologne-clouded back slaps.

My parents are first—my mom clinging to me like I've just returned from a hostage situation, my dad thumping me on the back like I just brought home a Lombardi trophy.

"That was incredible," my mom gushes. "Unbelievable. Your timing! Your presence! You get that from me, you know."

My dad scoffs. "From you? Please. She gets it from me. Remember my set at Cousin Vinny's retirement party? Had the whole room crying."

"They were laughing at you, Dad."

He shrugs. "Comedy is comedy."

Before I can get swallowed by the Great Parental Debate of 2025, Effie appears like divine intervention, linking her arm through mine.

"Alright, superstar. VIP meet and greet's waiting. Let's move."

She steers me down the hallway like she's guiding a drunk prom queen—past crew giving quick congrats, past Eddie muttering post-show notes to himself, past Franny, who's happily curled up in a security guard's lap like she owns the damn venue.

I scratch behind her ears. "You crushed it out there, Franny. Emmy-level restraint."

Her tail thumps lazily. No notes.

Effie tugs me forward. "No time for dog affirmations. You've got fans to delight."

The noise of the crowd still buzzes in my ears as we wind through corridors. I'm riding the high— warm skin, aching cheeks from smiling—but then I remember. Hunter. In the crowd.

I lean in. "By the way... Hunter's here."

Effie doesn't miss a step. Her grip tightens. Her eyes spark. She's already twenty moves ahead.

"Oh really?" she says, too breezy.

I narrow my eyes. "Effie."

She shrugs, mock-innocent. "Maybe you imagined it. Or maybe I imagined it. Or maybe we both imagined it, simultaneously, in the exact same way, because the universe is messy and dramatic and loves a callback."

I groan. "I hate you."

She grins. "You wish."

But there's no time to unpack her cryptic chaos, because the meet and greet door swings open, and I'm hit with another wave of applause, cheers, and the kind of starry-eyed devotion I'll never get used to.

For a second, Hunter isn't the most important thing in the room.

Despite everything, I light up. This part never gets old. I meet them—one by one—fans who paid for the privilege of a photo and a moment. And somehow, I still can't believe they want to meet me.

Some come bearing gifts: a framed poster of the tour, a t-shirt with my face on it, homemade merch with my signature phrase printed across the front:

"Listen, I didn't choose the drama life. The drama life chose me."

I hold up the shirt, laughing. "I should really start paying you guys for these."

A girl with pink hair beams. "Don't worry. We already started a bootleg merch shop."

I gasp. "You're *profiting off my pain?*"

She shrugs. "Capitalism, baby."

Effie snorts from the corner, Franny in her lap like a certified therapy dog. And honestly? She kind of is. Watching them both soak up attention like they were built for this life makes the weight pressing on my ribs loosen—just a little.

For a moment, I let it land: I'm here. I'm standing. I'm loved. That counts for something.

The line moves. Fan after fan. Hug after hug. Photo after photo.

And then—

The last person steps forward.

I barely glance up, reaching automatically for the playbill they're holding out. I'm in rhythm now. Muscle memory. Smile. Sign. Next.

"Who should I make it out to?"

I poise the Sharpie.

Silence.

Then a voice—low, familiar, wrapped in every memory I've been trying to outrun for the last seven years.

"Make it out to 'Asshole who let you go.'"

The Sharpie slips.

Time warps.

I force myself to look up.

Hunter.

Standing there like a punchline with perfect timing. Playbill in hand like he's just another fan, like he hasn't haunted me from the backseat of my own brain.

What spectacular timing. I just buried a marriage, and now here's the man I never fully grieved.

The man I shoved into a box labeled **Regret** and locked somewhere between **Almost** and **What If.**

And yet—here he is.

The room fades. The lights go dim. The air between us thickens with everything unsaid.

Because we weren't simple.

And we were never really finished.

And now, I have no idea what to say.

Chapter Twelve

I grip the Sharpie in my hand, but I don't move.

I just stare.

Hunter stands there, playbill still extended like this is a totally normal interaction. Like he's just another fan in line. Like seven years haven't passed. Like he didn't quietly wreck me.

My heartbeat skitters. My breathing's gone shallow. I'm supposed to say something. I always have the perfect line, the quick comeback, the disarming joke—but now?

Nothing.

Hunter doesn't look away.

Finally, after what feels like a lifetime crammed into a single second, he tilts his head slightly.

"You still sign autographs for people from your past?"

It snaps me out of the fog. My wit finds its footing.

I grab the playbill, flip it open, and without looking at him, scrawl across the page in big, looping letters:

No refunds. No exchanges.

Then I slap it against his chest.

Hunter catches it mid-fall. He glances down, reading—and dammit, he smiles.

It's barely there, just a flicker, but I feel it like a sucker punch to the ribs.

I square my shoulders. Focus. "So, what, you just show up at my shows now? You a fan?"

He tucks the playbill under his arm. "I was in the neighborhood."

I let out a dry laugh. "Albany's your neighborhood? Since when?"

Before he can answer, divine intervention arrives in the form of Effie.

"Oh, hey," she says, breezing in between us like she wasn't absolutely eavesdropping from behind the curtain. Franny trots in beside her, leash in hand. "Security usually kicks out weird men pretending to be fans, but I figured I'd let this one slide. For the drama."

"Effie," I hiss.

"What?" She shrugs. "I like to keep things interesting."

Franny, traitor that she is, immediately wiggles out of Effie's grip and makes a beeline for Hunter.

He crouches to meet her, rubbing behind her ears. "Well, nice to finally meet the real star of the show. Are you keeping your mom in line?"

Franny melts under his hands. That dopey golden retriever grin spreads across her face like she's never known betrayal.

Something sharp twists in my chest. I can't let her fall in love with him, too.

I cross my arms. "You should go."

Hunter straightens up. Meets my eyes.

And here it is.

The moment I've been dodging since I first spotted him in the crowd.

He should go. I'm telling him to go. So why isn't he moving?

He glances at Effie. "Can I have a minute?"

Effie raises a brow. "With her?"

He nods.

She considers him for a second, then shrugs. "Not my circus, not my monkeys."

She winks at me, whistles for Franny, and exits stage left, leaving me alone.

Alone with him.

A few caterers linger, quietly stacking chairs. Otherwise, it's just the two of us—and the ghost of everything we never said.

I exhale. "What do you want?"

Hunter doesn't flinch. "To talk."

I laugh, empty. "Now? After sneaking into my show like a groupie?"

"Hey," he says with a crooked smirk. "You signed my playbill. That makes me an official fan."

"Hunter."

The smile fades. His voice is lower now. Careful. "I saw you were coming to Albany. And I figured... if there was ever a time..."

My jaw clenches. And there it is—the anger I was missing earlier, rising like smoke.

"If there was ever a time?" I echo. "Is now—hours after my separation became a punchline—a good time?"

I look at him. Really look.

He's older. Sharper around the edges. The same boy I loved once, now dressed in grown-man skin and regrets.

And still—I feel it.

That tug.

The pull I've spent years denying.

I shake my head. "I can't do this. Not here. Not now."

He nods. Doesn't press. Doesn't move.

"Then when?" he asks quietly.

I don't have an answer. I hate that I don't have an answer.

"Hunter, it just... can't be here."

He swallows, turns toward the door. I can't tell if he's angry or sad or both. I just watch his hand tighten around the playbill like it's something sacred.

I'm still holding the Sharpie when Effie reappears, Franny in tow and her phone in the air like it's a winning lottery ticket.

"Oh, Char. I forgot to give you your phone," she announces, then slows as she takes in the lingering tension.

She frowns. "Well, looks like *someone* made progress—just kidding. What the hell even was that?"

I take the phone wordlessly. There's a lump in my throat I refuse to let become tears.

Effie watches me. "You okay?"

I don't answer.

Franny flops at Effie's feet, clearly exhausted from the emotional rollercoaster.

Effie crosses her arms. "Talk about what?"

I blink. "What?"

"You were staring at him like he was the grand prize in a rigged carnival game."

"Eff—"

"Look. Big night. Big emotions. Big... whatever *that* was. But you're going to talk to him, right?"

I hesitate. And then—my phone buzzes.

A single text. "I know here's not the right spot, but maybe we can talk over a drink tonight?"

I look up. He's standing by the exit, hands in his pockets, looking at me like he already knows my answer.

Effie exhales, already pulling on her coat. "I'll take Franny back to the hotel."

"I didn't say yes."

"You didn't have to."

I let out a soft, frustrated curse under my breath.

I shouldn't.

I really, truly shouldn't.

But my fingers are already moving. My breath catches. A pause. A beat.

And then:Where?

Chapter Thirteen

The bar he chooses is tucked into the corner of a quiet street, dimly lit with dark leather booths and an amber glow from the wall sconces. It's the kind of place where conversations stay private and drinks feel stronger than they are—like the kind of bar you take a secret to, just to see if it'll stay put.

Hunter is already there when I walk in, a whiskey in front of him, eyes locked onto me the second I step through the door. I tell myself it doesn't make my stomach twist.

I slide into the seat across from him, pulling off my coat.

"So," I say, leveling my gaze at him. "Why are you here?"

Hunter's mouth quirks like he expected that. "Albany's not exactly the vacation destination of choice, is it?"

I lift a brow. Waiting.

He exhales, fingers tapping against his glass. "Saw your show was here. Thought I'd stop by."

I scoff, reaching for the drink the bartender sets in front of me. "You drove from wherever you live just to say hi?"

Hunter doesn't flinch. "Yeah. I guess I did."

I smirk. "Where do you live, even?"

"Currently at home. But I'm moving to Chicago in a few weeks."

There's a silence between us. I take a sip, letting the burn settle before speaking. "I haven't seen you in seven years."

His lips press together like he's weighing the truth. "Not for lack of trying."

I glance away, tracing the rim of my glass. The truth is, I haven't let myself think about him in any way that mattered. Not deeply. Not safely. I was too busy keeping my head above water in a marriage already sinking.

But now that he's here—voice, presence, pull—that what-if I buried starts clawing its way back up like it never really died.

"So," I say, tilting my head. "Chicago?"

Hunter nods, stretching his arm across the back of the booth. "Got the call a few weeks ago. Counselor for the Bulls. It's what I always wanted."

"You're actually doing it," I say, and something in my voice tips between admiration and something else I'm not ready to name.

He watches me. "Took me long enough."

"Anyone special coming with you?"

His laugh is low, nearly bitter. "Nah. Just me. A few things here and there. Nothing serious." He tips his glass toward me. "You?"

I pause. "You saw the announcement."

"Hard to miss."

He doesn't ask why. Doesn't push. But I feel it—his eyes on me, heavy with questions he knows not to ask.

I sigh. "He was a piece of shit."

Hunter shakes his head. "I hate that I'm not surprised."

"Yeah?"

He shrugs, studying me like I'm something he once knew by heart. "That kind of success? Most men can't hold it without trying to shrink it."

I huff a quiet laugh. "Maybe I didn't even get it. Not really."

There's a beat.

Then he says, "You know, after you got married, my girlfriend at the time caught me looking at old photos of us. She lost it. Said I was obsessed."

"Were you?"

His jaw clenches. He doesn't answer.

I smile, slow. "Maybe you were onto something."

Hunter chuckles, but it doesn't erase the tension in his shoulders. "Can I ask you something, bird?"

"Of course."

"Are you that surprised?"

And there it is. The question I've been avoiding.

I swirl my drink. "As much as the text hurt, and his actions hurt, the truth is... we weren't building something real. When we got married, this was all a pipe dream. Then everything changed. The right moment hit, and my career took off like a rocket I didn't know I was sitting on.

One minute I was prioritizing him—the dinners, taking myself off birth control. The next, I was flying city to city, opening for women I used to idolize.

He was supportive... eventually. But maybe only after the checks started clearing. And maybe I clung to the idea of home more than I clung to him. That happens when your childhood is chaos. You just want somewhere soft to land."

I pause, let the silence settle. Then add, voice quieter: "But I never cheated."

Then I correct myself.

"Well. I did kiss you."

Hunter stills.

"I can't speak on your marriage," he says. "And I can't speak on Brian. I hate him because he got you, and I hate him because he blew it. But what I can say is—none of that excuses what he did. Not with you. Not with who you are now."

I take a long sip. "You always know what to say."

His lips twitch. "That's what I'm here for."

Our drinks are refilled. And somewhere between the second round and the way the night starts folding into itself, the air changes.

The flirting becomes real. His leg presses against mine. His hand grazes my knee. And when he laughs, it's like no time has passed at all.

"You ever think about what would've happened if things had been different?" I ask, breath catching.

He doesn't hesitate. "All the time."

My heart pounds.

I reach into my bag and slide a plastic keycard across the table.

Room 806.

He picks it up, turning it between his fingers. That slow smile spreads.

"Guess some things can be different."

We leave separately, but he follows. I step into the elevator. He gets on a few seconds later.

We don't speak. Just exist in the quiet hum between floors. My fingers brush his.

And when I open the hotel door, Franny barrels toward me like I've been gone for years.

Hunter laughs. "She truly has zero chill."

Franny throws herself at him too, a traitor to her core.

And when he stands—hands on my hips, eyes burning into mine—I whisper, "Let's do this right."

Then I kiss him.

And this time, neither of us pull away.

Chapter Fourteen

The hotel door clicks shut behind us.

And that's all it takes.

In one breath, he has me backed against the wall, his mouth crashing into mine like a wave breaking after years of stillness. It's not sweet—it's hungry. Hot. Like we're still eighteen, sneaking around in cars. I taste whiskey and adrenaline and the faintest trace of spearmint gum, and I know he tastes the same on me. We're breathing each other in, every exhale laced with alcohol and want.

There's no hesitancy.

No delicate undoing of buttons or soft glances seeking permission.

He peels my coat from my shoulders, slides his hands beneath the hem of my dress like he has every right. And maybe, in this moment, he does.

I groan when his fingers find my thighs—familiar territory explored with brand-new urgency. His hands are large, calloused, reverent. And then he presses his hips against me and I feel him—hard, thick, unmistakably ready—his cock against my leg, straining through his jeans like it's been waiting for this since college.

I grab at his shirt, yanking it over his head. He helps, impatient. We're not undressing each other. We're *unwrapping* what we've craved.

My dress falls to the floor. His jeans follow. My back hits the bed with a thud, and then he's over me, on me, everywhere. His fingers slide between my legs like he already knows what he'll find—wet. *Dripping.*

And when he slides two fingers into me?

I swear the room tilts.

My breath catches, hips rising to meet him like they remember exactly what he can do. He curls them just right—just like he used to. Like nothing's changed.

"Oh my God," I gasp, hand fisting in the sheets.

He leans down, lips brushing my jaw as he whispers, "Still fits me like a glove."

I let out something between a laugh and a moan. "Your ego is showing."

"So is your orgasm," he says, voice rough, fingers still working inside me—slow and deep and *knowing*. My thighs are shaking. My vision's going soft around the edges.

He watches me, eyes dark, focused, like he's memorizing the exact moment I come apart for him.

When it hits—hot and breathless and almost angry—I grab his wrist, gasping his name like a warning.

He doesn't stop until I'm panting, legs trembling, lips parted in disbelief.

And then he kisses me again—slower this time, messier. His hands cradle my face. His cock nudges against me, and I pull him in with my thighs, wordless.

When he finally thrusts into me, it's not just sex.

It's a return. A claiming.

A reminder that this thing between us never really disappeared—it just went dormant, waiting for the right night to light itself on fire again.

He moves with the rhythm of someone who knows me too well. Like he's been dreaming this. Like he's terrified it might vanish if we go too fast.

We don't talk. We don't need to. Because our bodies have always had perfect timing, even when the rest of us didn't.

And when we finish—shaking, breathless, a tangled mess of limbs and sweat and years of unspoken words—it doesn't feel like a mistake.

It feels like fate, finally keeping its promise.

The morning light filters through the heavy hotel curtains, casting a soft golden glow across the room. The sheets are warm, tangled around my bare legs, and my body aches in that sweet, tender way that only happens after really good sex. My skin smells like his cologne. Like last night. Like memory.

Hunter's arm is draped across my waist, his breathing slow and steady against the back of my neck.

I let myself stay still.

Just for a minute.

No camera flashes. No passive-aggressive emails from Eddie. No headlines dissecting my every move. Just this: the quiet thrum of morning, the rise and fall of his chest behind me, the way his fingers twitch slightly like he's still holding on to me in his sleep.

And maybe he is. I don't move. I don't dare.

Because if I move, the moment might crack. If I move, I'll have to reckon with the fact that I just slept with Hunter Maisley.

Correction: *fucked* Hunter Maisley. Gloriously. Recklessly. Completely.

My brain is still catching up to what my body already knows—that every part of last night was real. That his hands on me, his mouth, the way he moved inside me like he *remembered* me... it wasn't a dream or nostalgia or old chemistry. It was *us*, still sharp and present after all this time.

And that's what makes it harder.

Because it still feels good. Familiar. Safe. Which is almost cruel.

It's been forty-eight hours since my separation went public. Forty-eight hours since I learned the man I married was building a second life behind my back. And in that chaos, I reached for the one person I never truly let go of.

No regrets. That part's easy.

But clarity doesn't come with climax. And whatever last night was—it wasn't a solution.

I stare up at the ceiling. The light slants through the curtains in thin gold ribbons, painting the walls in soft, holy silence. It feels like a secret, this room. Like a pocket of time that shouldn't exist.

Hunter stirs behind me, his fingers brushing my stomach before he exhales a groggy breath. I feel the weight of him, the warmth. And it makes something tighten in my chest.

He's real. He's here. And I don't know what to do with that.

"Tell me this isn't a dream," he mutters, voice gravel-thick and sleep-warm.

I close my eyes. "I don't think dreams come with this much emotional fallout."

Hunter chuckles lightly and props himself up on his elbow, looking down at me. I feel his eyes before I meet them.

"You regret it?"

I shift onto my back, watching the ceiling again. "No. I knew what I was doing."

He waits. And I give it to him straight.

"But I also know I need space to figure things out. I haven't even slept in my own bed since the separation. I haven't opened my inbox or called my mom or... or decided if I'm getting a lawyer."

His expression is unreadable.

I sigh. "I don't want to drag you into the wreckage just because you showed up at the exact moment I needed someone familiar."

Hunter studies me for a long beat. Then he nods, slow and measured.

"I'm not asking for anything, Char. I just... I didn't want to let the moment pass again."

His voice is soft. Honest. And that makes it worse somehow. Because I know he means it. He brushes a strand of hair from my cheek. "We can wait. I've waited before. Let's just start at friendship. We're good at that."

A lump rises in my throat. "Yeah. We're good at that, huh?"

Hunter leans in, presses a kiss to my lips that's so gentle it nearly undoes me.

Then, like the universe couldn't resist a punchline —

Thud.

Franny launches herself onto the bed, tail wagging like she's missed all the drama and wants a rerun. Effie must have opened the share door on her way to the bathroom, without realizing there was a guest.

She flops directly between us and sighs, her body warm and heavy. We both start laughing, tangled limbs and too much history and one very pushy golden retriever between us.

"She's got great timing," I say, stroking her back.

"She's the only one who does," he jokes, pulling out his phone to film her.

I slip out of bed, tug on some clothes, and step into the bathroom. When I come back out, Hunter's already dressed, Franny's leash in hand.

He lifts an eyebrow. "What's one more walk through Albany together?"

I pause in the doorway.

This doesn't mean we're back. This doesn't mean we're anything.

But it means he showed up. When no one else did.

And right now, that feels like enough.

I nod.

"Yeah. One more."

Chapter Fifteen

Weeks have passed since my last show, and I've finally come home to Huntington Bay.

And it feels different now—like I'm seeing it for the first time. Maybe because, for the first time, I'm really here.

My house sits on two acres that kiss the edge of the Long Island Sound, the kind of place you fall in love with slowly and then all at once. On clear days, I can make out the faint silhouette of Connecticut across the water, like a mirage. It always reminds me of *The Great Gatsby*—that sense of longing, of something just out of reach. Except now, for the first time in a long time, I don't feel like I'm reaching. I'm just... here.

I bought this house last year. Brian hated the idea —he loved the one his parents bought us before the wedding, probably because there was no mortgage. But I wanted something that was mine. Just mine. And luckily, it is. The deed's in my name. There's something about that I hold close, like a secret I earned.

I had it decorated by an interior designer with very specific instructions: "coastal but not cheesy, serene but not sleepy, and nothing beige." They did a great job. Still, I only ever spent one Christmas here with my family. I was always too busy. Too booked. Too somewhere else.

But now? I'm here.

And I'm learning what it feels like to have a space that doesn't need to impress anyone. Just a space that holds me.

Most mornings, I wrap myself in a blanket and sit outside, watching the light ripple across the Sound. Franny barrels into the shallows like she's never seen the water before. She does it every day. It makes me laugh every time.

I know I should be grieving the end of my marriage, but there's not much to mourn when the foundation was hollow. Brian and I were never quite *in* it together. Two people side by side, not intertwined. More like background noise than a love story.

When I think back to our wedding, I remember a version of myself I don't recognize. A woman performing. Smiling on cue. Playing the role. I loved him, I think. I know I tried. But I also know I felt like I was acting the whole time.

Then my career took off. And suddenly, I didn't have to pretend anymore. And that's when everything quietly fell apart.

The divorce is being handled so seamlessly, it barely feels real. The lawyers move the papers. Eddie filters the emails. Effie keeps me distracted. And the headlines have already moved on to fresher gossip.

Brian didn't contest anything. No drawn-out arguments, no tug-of-war over the house or the dog or the narrative. Just a couple of signatures and the soft sound of a door closing.

I'm officially single.

And that, too, feels strange. Not heavy. Not devastating.

Just... light.

I always assumed that ending a marriage would feel like ripping something out by the root. But what if there was never anything growing there to begin with?

Honestly, I'm starting to feel grateful. Not just for the space and the silence—but for the version of myself that survived all of it. The version who carved out a career, a voice, a life, even while tethered to someone who never fully saw her.

And okay—if I'm being honest—some of that lightness comes from the fact that Hunter's back in my life.

We've stuck to our agreement: friends. Just friends.

The kind of friends who text constantly.

Hunter: Tried a new taco place today. Thought about you when they asked if I wanted extra hot sauce. I made the mistake of saying yes.
Me: Tell me you nearly died without telling me

you nearly died.

Hunter: There was sweating involved. Some light hallucinations.

Sometimes our conversations get deeper.

Me: Weird day. Got asked to do a panel about women in comedy. Super excited, but also kind of terrified?

Hunter: Terrified? You? You literally made a joke about your divorce while mid-divorce.

Me: Yeah, but this is a serious thing. People will expect wisdom.

Hunter: Then just be honest. Talk about the years it took to get where you are. How it wasn't just talent, but work. And remind them that you're still figuring things out, too. People don't need perfection. They just need something real.

And sometimes, it's quieter than that. Just the knowing he's out there. That if I call, he'll answer.

I'm not trying to label it. I'm not rushing toward anything. Not right now.

Because for the first time in a long time, I'm not afraid of being alone with myself. I'm not afraid of the stillness.

And the stillness? It's beginning to feel like peace.

It's a Saturday morning when Effie calls.

"You've been booked for a private gig in Chicago. Hosted at the United Center."

I arch an eyebrow. "Must be someone rich."

"Oh, you have no idea," she says, tone already two steps ahead.

Then she hangs up.

I glance at Franny, who's gnawing on a stick she probably dragged from the water.

"Well, road dog—looks like we're heading to Chicago."

She thumps her tail against the deck, completely oblivious to the fact that I have no idea what's waiting for me there. Or maybe—deep down—I do.

Chapter Sixteen.

The United Center hums with energy, even though it isn't full. It doesn't need to be. The magnitude of the space—its sheer size, the history it holds—swells inside me as I step through the backstage corridor. I've played sold-out arenas before, maxing out at fourteen thousand seats, but something about this night feels different. More intimate. More alive. Maybe it's the anticipation, or maybe it's something else entirely.

The stage is set at center court—just a stool, a mic, and a spotlight. Minimalist. Intentional. A stripped-down version of the usual flash and fire, but perfect in its simplicity. Tonight's audience isn't the typical crowd of screaming fans or critics scribbling in their notebooks. It's a closed event for the Chicago Bulls—the players, their families, coaches, and staff. A team-building experience, they'd called it. A moment of levity in the middle of a pressure-filled season.

I should be locked into the set I've been rehearsing all week, but my mind is elsewhere. As the car rolled through the city earlier, I pulled out my phone and hovered over a message. Just a simple note to let Hunter know I was here.

Me: Hey, I just landed in Chicago. Big private show tonight. Will you be around?

I expected nothing. Or maybe I expected everything. What I didn't expect was how fast he responded.

Hunter: Damn, I wish. I have a work event tonight.

I tried to play it cool, replying something breezy, brushing away the little pinch in my chest. But it lingered, no matter how much I tried to shake it off. I told myself it was fine—casual, friendly, no expectations. I told myself I wasn't disappointed. But that was a lie.

Now, with my mic in hand and the spotlight warming my skin, I take a breath. It's time.

"Well, well, well," I start, surveying the crowd. "A room full of professional athletes and their WAGs. I'm honored."

Laughter breaks across the seats like a wave.

I lean into the mic. "For those of you who don't know, WAGs stands for 'wives and girlfriends,' but honestly, we need a better name. I'm thinking MVPs—Motherfucking Viper Princesses—for dealing with your travel schedules, injury complaints, and groupie DMs."

The room lights up with laughter and applause. The women in the front row—glamorous, powerful, composed—whoop and clap. They're into it. And I ride the momentum, weaving jokes about sports injuries, late-night FaceTimes, and the contrast between professional athletes and the women who keep their lives upright.

And then a voice cuts through the crowd.

"Sounds like you're a bit bitter!"

It's loud. Teasing.

My stomach drops.

Because I know that voice. I'd know it in a crowd of thousands. And sure enough, I spot him halfway back, leaning casually in his seat like he's always belonged there.

Hunter.

My pulse stumbles. He wasn't supposed to be here.

But there he is—grinning, arms folded across his chest like this is just another night, just another show.

"Oh, I didn't realize hecklers were allowed at private events," I fire back, trying to keep my footing as the crowd oohs in delight.

Hunter shrugs. "Just figured I'd help keep you humble."

I smirk. "Hunter here thinks I'm humble," I say, then turn to the crowd. "He's been an audience member in my life for years, but this is his first time participating."

The arena erupts. The laughter is genuine and full, rolling over me like a tide. The jokes keep flowing, the back-and-forth sharp and easy. Every glance between us holds something deeper—something electric, familiar, and dangerous.

And then he stands.

For a second, I think he's leaving. My breath catches, the rhythm of the set faltering.

But he starts walking toward the stage.

"Okay," I say, laughing nervously as the players begin to cheer. "This is ridiculous—"

Hunter doesn't flinch. He reaches me, takes the mic, and turns to the crowd. "You think I'd let them out-hype me?" he says, eyes never leaving mine.

And then—he drops to one knee.

The arena explodes.

My brain shorts out. "What are you doing?" I hiss, panic blooming in my chest.

He lifts his shoulders, completely unbothered. "Relax, drama queen. I don't have a ring."

The laughter that follows is loud enough to shake the rafters.

"Then why are you down there?" I ask, my voice barely audible over the roar.

His eyes find mine, steady and warm. "Because I've loved you for most of my life," he says, "and I don't need a ring to tell you that."

The crowd quiets in an instant, like the whole room exhales at once.

I feel something crack open in my chest. He stays there, waiting—not performing, not joking—just present. And suddenly, I realize I don't want to run from this. I don't want to pretend this isn't everything I've been aching for.

"This is absolutely insane," I whisper.

Hunter's mouth curves. "You love it."

I do. God help me, I do.

"Fine," I say, letting the words roll out like surrender. "Get up, you dramatic idiot."

He does, but instead of brushing off the moment, he closes the distance between us in one long stride and kisses me.

It's not gentle. It's not tentative.

It's a years-long ache, poured into a kiss that tastes like everything we lost and everything we're reclaiming. His hands cradle my face, his mouth demanding and familiar, like he's been waiting since the second I left. The sound of the arena fades, replaced by the roaring in my ears, the press of his chest, the feeling of finally being found.

When we pull apart, breathless and dazed, he presses his forehead to mine. "Took us long enough, huh?"

I nod, eyes stinging. "Yeah. But we got here."

And we did.

It's not perfect. There's no ring. No clear next step.

But there's love. There's laughter. And there's us —standing in the middle of a basketball court, surrounded by strangers who are cheering like they've been rooting for us all along.

And somehow, it feels exactly right.

Not the ending of a show.

But the beginning of something real.

Something worth waiting for.

Something that—finally, finally—is ours.

Epilogue

There are moments in life that make you stop and wonder, *How did I get here?*—as if you've climbed a staircase in the dark and only now flicked on the light.

The first time you bomb on stage. The first time you don't.
The first time someone slips you a check just for making people laugh.
And, apparently, the first time your life detonates in full tabloid Technicolor... and the fallout turns out to be jet fuel.

Tonight, I'm standing in the wings of Studio 8H—home of *Saturday Night Live*—waiting for the red *LIVE* sign to ignite. The floor vibrates with controlled chaos: camera rigs rolling, wardrobe racks squeaking, someone shouting for more hairspray. Under other circumstances, my palms would be damp, my knees a little loose. But right now I feel steady—almost greedy for the spotlight—like the stage owes me something and I've come to collect.

Effie is pacing just behind me, phone in one hand, coffee in the other, managing chaos like it's oxygen. She has three assistants now, her own agency, and still refuses to let me walk into a show without a pep talk like it's our first open mic in a VFW basement.

"You got this," she mutters, like she's convincing herself more than me.

I glance at her, smirk. "I know."

Hunter's in the green room with our dog, Frankie —a mutt with satellite ears and strong opinions about skateboarders. He found her a year before Franny passed, and I swear Franny trained her in advance. It's like she knew I'd need someone to keep pace with my shadow.

The stagehand gives the signal. Thirty seconds.

Effie squeezes my arm. "Go be funny."

I breathe once. Then step into the light.

The applause rolls over me like a wave—hot, alive, sharp at the edges. I stand there a beat, just long enough to soak it in.

Then I raise a hand. "Okay, okay—settle down. This isn't my funeral."

Laughter. We're off.

"I can't explain how surreal this is. Hosting *SNL*? Me? The girl who once did a stand-up set in a Long Island pizzeria while an eight-year-old's birthday party screamed through the side room? At one point, I stopped mid-joke so they could sing Happy Birthday to Anthony."

More laughter.

"But here I am. Hosting *SNL*. And I know what you're thinking—'Wow, they'll really let anyone do this now.'"

Beat.

"And you're right. I mean, Pedro Pascal hosted last year and that man is too hot to be funny. You know what I mean? It's unfair. Let us have one thing, Pedro!"

Laughter builds, comfortably. I let it breathe.

But honestly, it's been a wild ride. Seven years ago, my life blew up in spectacular fashion when I found out my husband was cheating on me. And I know, I know—tragic. But let me tell you, it was the best thing that ever happened to me. Mainly for my bank account.

Seriously, I was out here trying to be a struggling comedian, and then—boom—one divorce, a couple of Netflix specials, and suddenly, I'm paying off my student loans early. Who knew heartbreak was the best business plan?

Pause. Let them laugh.

But yeah, my career took off because of my divorce jokes, and now? I'm happily remarried, which, uh... isn't as good for material. It's a real problem.

I married a man I knew in college. We reconnected, fell in love, and—ugh—it's actually healthy. I mean, what am I supposed to do with that? Get on stage and be like, 'Hey guys, ever been in a relationship where you communicate and feel emotionally safe?' Boring!

But, you know, it's been good for the soul not harboring that bitterness. And probably my blood pressure.

Cue dramatic piano chord from the band.

I pause. Look around. "Uh... what was that?"

Bowen Yang slides onto the stage in full Phantom-of-the-Opera drama—cape, gloves, candle, the whole unhinged Broadway package.

BOWEN (singing, Broadway-style):
"Ohhh, you're not bitter anymore?? What a tragedy, what a loss!
Who are you if not fueled by rage?? Should we send you back to your ex for the content??"

I blink. "Bowen. This is my cold open."

BOWEN (ignoring me, dramatically):
"Bitterness made you FAMOUS, it paid your RENT!
Now you're in loooove, but at what expense?!"

Cue Ego Nwodim in a floor-length gown, holding a prop contract.

EGO (singing):
"The Netflix deal was CLEARLY built on HATE!
But now you have—ugh—happiness? Great." *(eye roll)*

I look straight into the camera. "Okay, I feel attacked."

The lights dim. The full cast appears behind them, swaying like they're about to break into *Les Mis*.

BOWEN (final dramatic note):
"So take back your joy, your love, your peace!
But just know—we want that BITTERNESS BACK... at LEAST!"

The music cuts. They freeze in place, theatrical and tragic.

Long pause.

I turn to the audience, deadpan. "I would like to formally apologize for my personal growth."

Laughter erupts. The band kicks in. The cast breaks their pose.

I grin. "We've got an amazing show! Boygenius is here! So stick around—we'll be right back!"

The applause roars. The camera zooms out. Music plays. And as I step offstage, the world softens around me.

Hunter's waiting in the wings, arms folded, his signature smirk already forming.

"Don't say it," I warn.

He grins. "You crushed it."

I roll my eyes, but my chest is full. He reaches out, touches my cheek, then presses a quick kiss to my lips.

"Proud of you," he whispers, soft and sure.

And just like that, it hits me. The arc. The entire, beautiful climb.
This moment. This life. This love.
I didn't stumble into any of it.

I built it.

And just like that—we're live.

www.ingramcontent.com/pod-product-compliance
Lightning Source LLC
Chambersburg PA
CBHW070931250626
47159CB00009B/3204